MURDER
AT THE
MAGIC
ACADEMY

ALICIA RADES

ALSO BY ALICIA RADES

HIDDEN LEGENDS: ACADEMY OF MAGICAL CREATURES

The Fire Prophecy

The Water Legacy

The Earth Legend

The Air Omen

The Elemental War

The Soul Sacrifice

HIDDEN LEGENDS: COLLEGE OF WITCHCRAFT

The Coven's Secret

The Reaper's Shadow

The Cauldron's Curse

The Demon's Spell

The Warlock's Trial

The Witch's Fate

HIDDEN LEGENDS: PRISON FOR SUPERNATURAL OFFENDERS

The Villain Institute

The Criminal Lair

The Infernal Underground

The Assassin's Destiny

The Devil's City

The Elven Gate

Vengeance and Vampires

Ravenite

Resilience

Resolute

Retribute

Sea of Mermaid Secrets

Deep Waters

Rising Tides

Crashing Waves

Crystal Frost

Fire in Frost

Desire in Frost

Inspired by Frost

Fading Frost

Davina Universe

Divine Fate Trilogy:

Chosen by Grace

Touched by Grace

Awakened by Grace

Divine Descendants Duology:

Concealing Magic

Exposing Magic

CHAPTER 1

I always knew when something bad was going to happen, and the dark storm clouds brewing above Thornshire only intensified the chill creeping down my spine. I'd lived in a town full of witches all my life, yet Halloween never failed to give me the creeps.

"There's nothing to be afraid of, Elodie." I spoke the words out loud, as if the sound of my own name might help convince me.

Although the eerie feeling told me I should be cautious, I didn't *trust* the instinct. I had to believe the hairs rising on my arms were a result of the brisk weather and not an ominous warning. This wouldn't be the first time my intuition was wrong. Even if this sensation *meant* something, I had no further clues to decipher its significance.

I steeled my nerves. I wasn't scared to walk across campus on my own. I'd show anyone who wanted to hurt me what my magic was capable of.

Which made this unsettling feeling in my gut... strange.

I shivered as I stepped out of my dorm hall and into the cool autumn air. I'd dressed as Red Riding Hood in a short red dress with a black corset, long black tights, and a velvet red cloak. I wasn't exactly dressed for the weather, but Luna and I would be spending most of our night indoors, partaking in the Halloween festivities on campus.

I attended Thornshire Academy, a university for witches founded hundreds of years ago when our witch ancestors migrated to the states. Here, witches learned to harness their powers for brewing potions, communing with spirits, forging wands, and casting powerful spells. All witches in Thornshire attended the academy, because learning our magic was equally a part of our religion—in which we honored our ancestors in the afterlife—as it was important to our economy. We were one of the top cranberry exporters in all of the New England area, and it was our magic that kept the bogs producing high-quality fruit at such a fast rate.

I was in my first year at the academy, but my older cousin Luna would graduate next semester. She'd promised to hand down all her campus knowledge before graduation. Tonight, she was my guide to all the best Halloween parties on campus.

Halloween was always a big to-do in Thornshire. Townspeople decorated their homes with strings of orange lights, massive lawn displays depicting giant skeletons, and oversized blow-up spiders. Businesses competed for the best window displays by enchanting cauldrons to light up and bubble or using necromancy magic to make skeletons wave at passersby. Farmers brought their biggest pumpkins to the town square, and a prize was awarded to the largest one, which always weighed over a thousand pounds. Cider tastings and hayrides were everywhere, along with ghost tours at various historical locations.

On campus, the theater department hosted a haunted house in the university's main academic building—Haunted Halls, they called it. I'd been there with Kylan a few times in high school, when we were still dating. It'd been a lot of fun, and the event only got better every year.

My heels clicked on the sidewalk as I crossed the quad toward Luna's dorm. Around me, tall Victorian structures towered several stories. Four dorm buildings that housed thousands of students faced one another to form a square, and a big lawn stretched between them. Usually, the quad was bustling with activity, but everyone must've already been at their parties, because I was alone.

I'd been running late, which Luna normally *hated*, but she'd messaged me earlier saying she was running behind as well. I checked my phone to see if she'd sent any updates, but she hadn't. It was almost ten o'clock, which was still early by witch standards, but Haunted Halls had already been open for hours. Luna and I had to get going soon or we'd miss the best festivities in the countdown to the witching hour.

As I slid my phone back into my crossbody bag, I caught sight of movement in the shadows. A breeze swept across the quad, making the hairs on the back of my neck stand straighter. I reached for my wand in my bag. If someone thought they'd pull a Halloween prank by scaring a girl like me, they could think again.

A black cat emerged from the shadows, skittering beneath the light of a streetlamp. I slowly released my grip on the wand. It was only Halloween, and I couldn't let something as simple as a black cat freak me out.

Though… a black cat crossing your path was never a good sign.

I pulled my cloak tighter around me, shooting one last glance around the quad. There was nothing there. I had to get to Luna's dorm room quickly, because she'd talk me down and convince me this was nothing to worry about.

I hurried into her dorm building. Luna's room was located on the first floor at the end of the hall. She was the resident advisor for her dorm and had one of the best rooms on campus, complete with a living room and kitchenette. She even had a fireplace she usually kept burning.

As I passed by the other rooms, my gaze locked on one door in particular. Unease twisted in my stomach, though it was entirely unrelated to the strange feeling I'd gotten outside. Kylan lived in this hall, and the last thing I wanted was to run into him. I'd seen him on the broomball field a few weeks ago when I was crossing campus. Broomball was a lot like soccer, only played on flying brooms. Kylan had been so focused on scoring a goal I didn't think he'd seen me that day, and I'd done my best to avoid him ever since.

I hurried past his room and stopped at Luna's door on the end. I knocked, but no answer came, which was weird because she was expecting me. I tried the door handle, and it twisted easily. "Luna?"

I was met only with resounding silence. When she said

she was running behind, I figured she was deep in some class project like she always was and needed the extra time to get into her costume. If there was one thing that could make Luna lose track of time, it was her academics. I didn't realize she wouldn't be here when I arrived.

But then again, Luna wouldn't leave her dorm room without locking it... She must be around. She was probably just blasting haunting music in her earbuds like she did when she studied.

I called her name louder and stepped inside. An icy chill hit me, even though there were coals still glowing in the fireplace. The doors to the bedroom and the bathroom were both open, but the lights were off inside both of them. A sitting area circled the fireplace in the living room, with a long couch situated with its back facing the door.

"Very funny, Luna," I teased as I approached the sitting area. "It's not like you to fall asleep when we have plans—"

My words halted in their tracks when I caught sight of black heels pointed up toward the ceiling near the base of the couch. My heart lurched as I raced around the furniture to see Luna sprawled out across the floor. She wore a brown trench coat with a Sherlock Holmes hat askew atop her head. Her wand lay in one of her limp, outstretched hands.

"Luna!" I cried.

I dropped to my knees beside her and frantically shook her, but she remained unresponsive. Her skin appeared dull and sickly... a color I'd only seen once before. Luna remained entirely motionless, though I pleaded with our ancestors to show me the rise and fall of her chest. My prayers remained unanswered.

I pressed my fingers to the side of her throat in search of a pulse, but the all-encompassing devastation that slammed into my gut told me everything I already knew but refused to believe. This couldn't be happening again. Not to Luna.

The pulse I so desperately searched for wasn't present.

I staggered to my feet as the dread I'd felt when crossing the quad intensified into something far more sinister and horrible. The grim reaper himself might as well have curled his bony fingers around my throat, because it felt as if my terror might just rip my soul from my body right alongside Luna's. The edges of my vision blurred, and I found myself gasping for breath.

I hadn't been imagining things when I said that something bad was going to happen. Not this time. My cousin was dead, and no amount of psychic visions or cryptic warnings from beyond could save her now.

I stumbled toward the fireplace and caught myself on the mantle. For the briefest of moments, an image of flames flashed across my vision. I saw the edges of paper burning to embers, before my very real, harrowing reality came back into focus. Fingers trembling, I tore my gaze from Luna's body to peer into the fireplace.

A tiny piece of paper no larger than a quarter was wedged in the corner, far away from the embers. I bent to inspect it. I took special care to lift the paper so that it wouldn't crumble into ashes. The edges were burnt, but I was able to make out a singular phrase typed out in small letters.

Murder in Thornshire.

Usually, my psychic abilities weren't so direct, but this vision had been unmistakable. Whatever Luna had burned earlier had been incredibly important.

And it might just be what got her killed.

CHAPTER 2

I called the police, and I knew I didn't have much time before they arrived. If Luna's spirit was still hanging around, I had to talk to her to find out what happened here. Most ghosts of the recently departed were scared and confused. She wouldn't want to talk to strangers, but she'd talk to me—if I managed to get through to her.

Witches knew better than to stick around on an earthly plane for too long, because spirits could become trapped here. It was better to cross to the afterlife as soon as possible, which made it harder to contact them, though not entirely impossible. When spirits couldn't appear in full form, they communicated through psychic visions. The problem was interpreting those visions in a way that made any sense.

All the supplies I needed to conduct a séance were already laid out upon her altar. Every witch at Thornshire

Academy had an altar in their room fully stocked with cedar bundles, crystals, candles, and tarot cards.

I pinched the candle wick between my fingers, and it lit at my command. Using the flame I created, I lit the cedar bundle to cleanse the room of negative energies. Then I placed three amethyst crystals around the altar. Finally, I went to the fridge and found an apple—honeycrisp, Luna's favorite. I placed that beside the candle as an offering.

I knelt beside the altar, forcing my tone to remain steady. "Luna, if you're still here, make your presence known."

I waited for a sign from beyond, but the room remained silent. Not so much as a breeze passed by. Real séances weren't like in the movies. Ghosts *could* appear to witches in full ethereal form, but only under the best of circumstances. Most séances resulted in fragmented messages, which could come from unintended messengers. It wasn't a perfect spell, but I needed to try it. If Luna could shed any light on what happened here, this was her chance.

I continued. "I received a vision of your fireplace. You sent me that message, didn't you? You wanted me to know about a murder in Thornshire. Were you talking about your own?"

I paused to await her response, but nothing came.

"Luna, I need more information," I urged. "If you recall anything about what happened to you tonight, you can tell me now and I'll pass that information on to the police."

I glanced around the room, hoping to see Luna's spectral outline somewhere in the corner. Even if she had no messages to share, I at least wanted to say goodbye.

But Luna didn't show up.

This felt all too familiar, but I couldn't go back down the road of wondering why someone I loved wouldn't show up to say goodbye. My magic simply wasn't strong enough to bring her spirit to me.

"I'm sorry I was running late, Luna. I should've been here sooner." I hoped Luna heard my apology. I hoped she felt it as deep in her spirit as I meant it.

A loud *thud* sounded from behind me. I startled so quickly that I sprang to my feet and whirled around. Air billowed around the end of my cloak, blowing the candle out.

Across the room at the kitchenette, a stack of textbooks had fallen off the counter and lay scattered across the floor. My racing heart slowed as I crossed the room to pick them up.

As I was arranging the textbooks back into their stack, I noticed an orange piece of paper only a few inches long. I picked it up to see the words *Haunted Halls* sprawled across it in big bold letters. It was a ticket to the haunted house on campus. At first, I thought it had to be from last year, but then I noticed today's date listed at the bottom.

That was strange, because Luna and I had been planning to attend Haunted Halls together later tonight. Tickets were sold at the door, so I didn't know what she was doing with a ticket here in her room.

The door burst open, and three burly police officers raced into the room with their wands raised. The man in front was tall and middle-aged, with a sheriff's badge glinting off his uniform.

"Clear!" the sheriff called as he lowered his wand. Several other officers, along with a man wearing a jacket labeled *coroner* stepped into the room.

The sheriff's concerned gaze flickered toward Luna's body, but he kept his attention on me. "You're the one who called?"

I nodded. I recognized him, but he didn't seem to remember me. I wasn't surprised. My face had been one of hundreds in a mourning crowd of high schoolers the last time I saw him.

I shoved those memories aside, because I needed to focus right now. Though, the familiarity of it all kept those memories bubbling up faster than I could push them to the back of my mind. I had to keep them from spilling over, just long enough to talk to the officers. Then I'd allow myself to break down.

"I'm Elodie Graves," I told the sheriff. "I'm Luna's cousin. She asked me to meet her here so we could walk to Haunted Halls together. I found her like this and called the police right away."

"Elodie," he repeated kindly. "I'm Sheriff Woodfield. We're going to take care of everything, all right?"

He was trying to calm me down, but the sight of Luna lying there motionless made me want to hurl. One of the officers was already snapping photos of the scene, and another knelt down to check for a pulse. As expected, he found none.

"There are no visible injuries," a deputy with a mustache said.

A third officer had gone over to the window to inspect it. "No signs of forced entry, either."

The coroner knelt beside Luna to begin inspecting her body. He gently tugged down on her collar, and my body gave a shudder at the sight of black veins spiderwebbing up her chest and across her collarbone. "The cause of death is clear, Sheriff."

I'd heard of curses like this, but I'd never seen it before. Luna had been killed by some sort of dark magic, like someone had done this *intentionally*. Only the cruelest of witches would ever dare cast such a curse.

Sheriff Woodfield glanced around at the tidy space. "There's no evidence here to indicate a struggle. It's possible she was alone at the time of death."

"She couldn't have been," I insisted.

The sheriff's gaze darted to the wand in Luna's hand. I could tell by the calculating look on his face that he was already forming theories. "Did you witness someone else at the scene?"

I shook my head. "No, but if you're suggesting she did this to herself, you're wrong. Luna just secured her internship at the Records Hall. It was her life-long dream to become a curator of spell books and magical artifacts. She wouldn't just give that up."

"I assure you that we're very good at our jobs, Miss Graves," the sheriff said. "We're going to find out what happened here, and we won't be jumping to any conclusions until we've gathered *all* the evidence. I was merely suggesting a possibility. But you're correct, we can't know what happened until we conduct a full investigation. Would you mind stepping out into the hall with me?"

I knew what he was doing. He wanted to question me before I broke down—or blew up. I understood it was part of his job, but I found myself rooted in place. "Please, Sheriff. Let me stay long enough to see how it happened. You do have a spell that will reveal her last moments, don't you?"

I hadn't seen it done before, but I'd heard the police used a similar spell the night of the Enchanted Ball. It was extremely advanced magic, something only a few witches in the coven could cast.

Sheriff Woodfield hesitated. I didn't think civilians were usually allowed to witness this kind of thing, but he must've grown sympathetic to the desperation in my eyes. It was like he knew what leaving this room without answers would do to me, because he nodded. "I really shouldn't be doing this, but I'll make an exception this one time."

He drew his wand from the holster on his belt. He aimed it at Luna's corpse and muttered an incantation under his breath. Tendrils of sparkling blue magic swirled out of his wand, wrapping around Luna's form. Before my eyes, a spectral image of her appeared hovering in the air. It wasn't her spirit, as the apparition was only about a foot tall, like a shrunk-down version of her—a mere memory projected into the air like a hologram.

The projection of Luna was dressed in her Sherlock Holmes outfit, only her cheeks were brighter in color. She wore a confident expression, appearing oblivious to what was about to transpire. The miniature version of Luna lifted her wand straight out in front of her.

"I'm a strong witch." Her voice filled the room, and I nearly crumbled to my knees at the sound of it, though it wasn't *quite* right. There was an ethereal note to her voice, indicating the spell working its magic. "I can do this."

Then the specter of Luna spoke an incantation. A bright light flashed across the room the same time a powerful gust of wind blasted the image of Luna back. The wind appeared only in the vision, but the light was blinding. I shielded my eyes, but when I opened them again, the vision of Luna was gone.

The room had gone quiet, and I hated that the officers said *nothing*.

"That's it?" I demanded. "You need to go back further to see if anyone was in the room with her!"

The sheriff frowned. "I'm afraid the spell can only reveal the last few moments before death. From what we saw here, it appears Luna cast this curse upon herself."

"She wouldn't!" I cried.

"No one is suggesting she did this on purpose," the sheriff assured me. "It seems your cousin was dabbling in magic she shouldn't be and her spell backfired. You said she planned to pursue a career in the Records Hall—a scholar, if you will. It's reasonable to assume she had no ill intent and this was merely research for her."

"Luna was a researcher through and through, but she would *never* do a spell she wasn't trained for." My hands began to curl into fists, until I recalled the paper I'd found in the fireplace. I stopped myself before I could damage it, and held it up. "I found this. It says *murder in Thornshire*. Isn't that suspicious? Luna was trying to tell us something."

"We'll admit it into evidence." The sheriff sounded intrigued, though not entirely convinced. He called one of his officers over with an evidence bag, and I dropped the burnt piece of paper inside. "Did you witness anything else?"

"Just this." I showed him the ticket I'd found. "Luna had a ticket for Haunted Halls, but we were planning on going together. I'm not entirely sure it's hers."

One thing was for certain. The vision only showed a partial truth. I didn't believe for a second that Luna was alone when this happened. Somebody did this to her. If this ticket belonged to the killer, then the suspect had come straight here from Haunted Halls. The police could use security footage to narrow the suspect list.

Sheriff Woodfield placed the ticket into another evidence bag, but his tone was dismissive. "Thank you, Miss Graves. We'll take it from here."

I furrowed my brow. "You don't believe me?"

"We're prepared to conduct a full investigation, and the evidence will reveal the truth. We'll let you know what we find. In the meantime, is there anyone we can call to walk you back to your room?"

The thought of being around *anyone* right now churned my guts, because I already knew it wouldn't help. My parents would try to get me to talk about it, but right now I just needed a moment alone to grieve before everyone started hounding me with questions.

Luna was a different story. She shouldn't be alone right now, even if her spirit was no longer attached to her body.

I shook my head. "I can walk myself back, but you should call Luna's parents. They need to know what happened here."

He nodded firmly. "We will. Take care of yourself, Elodie."

The officers basically ignored me as they turned back to the coroner. I caught sight of a black body bag, and I knew I couldn't stick around to watch them carry her away.

I did the worst thing I could possibly do. I left Luna alone.

And I fled.

CHAPTER 3

I felt wholly detached from my body as I hurried out of the room. A group of students had gathered down the hall. My gaze darted their way for a mere second. Like magnets drawn toward one another, my eyes locked on Kylan's blue irises. I could swear those icy blue eyes could pierce their way into my soul. I quickly tore my gaze away and pulled my cloak hood over my head.

I turned my back on Kylan and sprinted toward the nearest exit. The air outside seemed colder than ever before, yet somehow I barely felt the bite of the wind. I was halfway across the quad when I heard the sound of my name.

"Elodie!"

My heart gave a start. That voice once brought so much warmth and comfort to my chest, but now it just made me want to run and hide. I kept on walking with my head down, because I couldn't face him right now.

"Elodie, please!" Kylan's strong hand landed on my

shoulder, and I whirled around to shove him off. His sandalwood scent surrounded me. For the briefest of moments, his touch ignited a fire in my belly, but the second I pulled away, the flame was gone.

I dared to look up at him, and my pulse skipped a beat. He wore jeans and a flannel shirt with a wolf-ear hat and matching fingerless fuzzy gloves. It struck me how ironic it was that he'd chosen a Big Bad Wolf costume the same night I dressed as Red Riding Hood. It seemed intentional, though there was no way he could've known.

I took a step back, my tone hollow. "Luna's dead."

"I heard. You shouldn't be alone." He was so soft and caring. It made it really hard to walk away. I just wanted to fall into those familiar arms and listen to him tell me everything would be okay, but after what happened between us, it wouldn't be the same anymore.

"I need time to process this," I insisted. "They say Luna killed herself in some magical accident."

"You don't believe them." Kylan wasn't asking. He knew me too well.

I shook my head. "How can I? Luna would never perform this kind of magic."

"What kind of accident, exactly?" Kylan wondered. "Was it the Deluge?"

The Deluge was a magical phenomenon all witches were warned of since birth. We were all born with magical abilities that grew with us as we aged, until we could wield enough power in young adulthood to cast bigger spells and attend the academy. Young spellcasters could only handle so much magic at once. The Deluge occurred when a young witch or warlock overloaded oneself with magic, resulting in illness or death. That's why we trained at the academy, so we learned how to manipulate our magic safely. The Deluge wasn't an issue after graduation, once a witch learned how to control their powers.

"Luna was killed by a dark curse," I told Kylan. "The sheriff did a spell to reveal her last moments before death, and it looked like she cast the curse but it backfired on her. Call me crazy, but my gut says there's more to the story. I knew something bad was going to happen... and this time it really did."

Kylan's eyes grew wide. "You need to trust your gut, Elodie."

I was taken aback. "The last time I trusted my gut, everyone said I was overreacting. Katie and Riley won't even talk to me anymore after what happened."

"*I* believe you." Kylan glanced around the quad nervously, but we were alone. Still, he lowered his voice. "About half an hour ago, I heard a scream. I opened my door to see what was going on, and I saw a masked man walking toward the stairwell. I figured Luna and her boyfriend must've got into a fight again. Everyone in our hall witnessed the screaming match they got into last week. It looked like she got rid of him, though, so I assumed she was fine."

"You have to go tell the police!" I demanded. "They may not be convinced by the evidence I found, but your eyewitness testimony proves someone else was there tonight. Luna and Aster broke up last week, and if he's mad enough about that, it gives him motive."

"I spoke to an officer in the hall, but they heavily implied that a masked man on Halloween isn't exactly suspicious. They said they'd take note of the scream I heard, but it isn't enough. I couldn't confirm for certain that the scream was hers, and even though I *thought* the masked man was coming from Luna's dorm, I didn't actually see him come out of her room. You really think it could be Aster?"

"I'm not sure," I admitted. "Luna seemed really devastated about the break-up, but I didn't prod. If Luna really cast this spell, then she did it in self defense. Which means that whether she died by her own spell or not, someone came here tonight to harm her."

"You said you found evidence in her room," Kylan pointed out. "What'd you find?"

I sighed. If the police didn't believe me, Kylan wouldn't. "Does a psychic vision count?"

"In court? No. To me? I'll believe anything you say, Elle."

The sound of my old nickname nearly knocked the breath out of me. Kylan didn't visibly react, and I realized he didn't even notice he said it.

I needed *someone* to believe me. "I saw a vision of something burning in Luna's fireplace. I found a burnt paper with a single phrase on it: *Murder in Thornshire.* The sheriff said they'd admit it into evidence, but he didn't seem convinced it was related."

Kylan furrowed his brow. "That doesn't sound unrelated at all. It sounds concerning."

I frowned. "You're the only one who thinks so."

"You have an innate psychic ability many spellcasters can never access. What do *you* think happened?"

All witches shared the same powers, but each one of us excelled in specialized areas. As my powers grew over the last few months, it'd become clear my specialty was clairvoyance. Kylan, on the other hand, had shown promise in alchemy. Potion making was far cooler than psychic visions that only led to horror.

The hairs on the back of my neck stood when I thought of the words I'd found in Luna's fireplace. "I think Luna was murdered," I admitted.

"If the police write this off as an accident, then Luna's killer goes free. Someone has to stop him."

I understood what Kylan was suggesting, and it was too much to ask. "You want me to solve my cousin's murder?"

"I'm saying that if the police don't like the evidence we presented, we're going to have to show them evidence they can't ignore."

"What exactly do you expect me to do?"

"I expect you to act like the Elodie I know. That girl would take action. She'd do whatever it takes."

I shook my head. "I'm not the same girl anymore."

"You're still in there somewhere. I know it, Elle. We don't have to stop being ourselves because we lost Emerson—"

"Don't you *dare* bring him up right now," I sneered. The sound of my old friend's name felt like a dagger to the gut.

"He was my friend, too. I'm not saying things haven't changed, because I know none of us will ever be the same again. But I don't want to see you lose yourself to it. What happened to going on to grad school to become an Intuit?"

Intuits were one of the most highly regarded professions in the coven. They were specialized psychics who used visions to counsel clients, like the coven's version of a psychiatrist. I'd wanted to become an Intuit for the longest time, but once I got the academy, I declared a major in astrology. It was only a four-year degree, opposed to the eight needed to become an Intuit.

Kylan didn't understand. I couldn't even help myself. How could I counsel other people?

"I have to be realistic," I told him.

"Aren't our lives strange enough as it is? People our age shouldn't see this much death, Elodie. I know our relationship is over and it's not my place to care about you anymore, but believe it or not, I don't want you to stumble upon another dead body. We need to stop this before another person we love ends up dead." Kylan reached out a hand. "What do you say? Are you with me?"

I stared down at his open palm. "I don't think we can work together on this."

"I believe you, Elle, and I'm the only one that does, but I'm not asking you to trust me. I'm asking you to trust *yourself.* Your psychic abilities are better than anyone I know, so if you say something's wrong here, then *something's wrong.* Let's prove that your intuition was right all along."

A siren blared over the quad, and the sound brought back horrible memories that made me want to run for cover. I turned to see the coroner wheeling a body bag outside. My arms curled around my middle as sickening images flashed through my mind. The sight of Luna's dead body would forever be seared into my memory.

Only this time, for the briefest of moments, I pictured Kylan lying there instead. Luna's death was enough to crush me—enough to send me crawling back to my room and praying for a spell that would undo what happened here tonight, even if no such magic existed.

But the thought of Kylan being next? *That* was enough to drive me forward, because Kylan was right about one thing. I couldn't stumble upon another dead body. Not if I could do something to stop it.

We had nothing to go off of but a message in Luna's fireplace and my psychic intuition, but I was certain someone had killed Luna.

And I had to stop them before they struck again.

"I'm in," I stated firmly. "You thought you saw Aster leaving Luna's dorm, and I found a ticket to Haunted Halls in her room. Aster's working at Haunted Halls tonight as one of the actors. Let's go see if he's our masked killer."

CHAPTER 4

Kylan and I walked across campus until we came upon the Academic Center, which housed most of our lecture halls and the campus cafeteria. Two tall towers with pointed peaks rose on either side of the entrance.

We paid for our tickets, then entered the building. The lights were off, and a grayish blue hue filled a long entry hall. The room was eerily silent, apart from creaks and distant moans of actual ghosts. Cobwebs hung from the chandelier and all over the walls. On a table sat a crystal ball, which projected creepy images of ghostly faces inside it. A potion bubbled inside a cauldron set over a burning fireplace. The sound of scurrying footsteps met my ears, and I jumped when the skeleton of a dead mouse skittered in front of us. Instinctually, I grabbed Kylan's arm, squeezing him close to me.

"It's only necromancy," Kylan assured me softly.

I quickly dropped his arm. Kylan and I hadn't been

together for months, but being this close to him felt natural.

It shouldn't.

I straightened my spine. "Right. Nothing to be afraid of."

Kylan kept on walking, and I followed. We came upon a sign at the other end of the hall that read, *Choose Your Adventure*. Three arrows pointed in different directions. One hallway was marked *Torture Chamber*, and we could hear screams of terror coming from that wing. The arrow pointing toward the cafeteria read *Death Cemetery*, and the final hallway was labeled *Monster's Lair*.

I pointed toward the *Monster's Lair*. "Aster should be working down there. He mentioned it a few weeks ago when I met him and Luna for lunch."

Kylan didn't move right away. "Are you sure you want to go down there? Torture's a bit of a heavy theme considering the coven's history, don't you think?"

I knew he was talking about more than the witch trials our people were subjected to hundreds of years ago. He wasn't sure I could handle it, considering what I'd witnessed tonight. I had no doubt this haunted house was full of all kinds of blood, gore, and horrible imagery that I didn't want to see. It wasn't going to stop me, though, not when my cousin's killer was still out there.

"There's a reason our people gravitate toward darker themes," I pointed out. "Exploring dark themes in a setting where it's all pretend allows us to dig deep into the human psyche. Things like this haunted house help people make sense of these terrible things like death, grief, and horror when it's too much to face in the real world."

"As long as you want to keep going, I'll be right here beside you. We can leave anytime you want."

"I'll be okay," I promised. "Let's go see what monsters we can find."

We only got a few feet before we found writing on the wall made to look like it was written in blood.

Innocent humans beware
Of what lurks in the monster's lair
Your minutes starts now; you have but five
Hurry if you wish to make it out alive

We entered a pitch-black hallway. We couldn't see anything, and I listened closely for any signs of monsters, which I knew were just students dressed up in costumes. Summoning real monsters would put the students at risk.

We must've tripped a sensor, because a strobe light flickered, and the actors began screaming. Beside us, someone dressed like a werewolf stood at an open class-room doorway, which was covered with bars like a cage. They howled like a dog and shook the bars. Above us, a student dressed as a giant spider used magic to hover themselves on the ceiling. Their costume legs twitched.

I found myself shrinking toward Kylan once more. He took my hand in his—those strong but gentle hands that used to touch me in places no one else had ever touched before. My cheeks heated at the memories. I didn't pull away from him as he continued leading me down the hall.

Students dressed in demon masks and others with glowing red eyes jumped out at us.

I leaned into Kylan. "Do you recognize any of these masks?"

"No. The guy I saw was wearing something more like a hockey mask, but I only saw a glimpse before he was gone. It could've been a skeleton mask."

"If it was Aster you saw leaving Luna's dorm, he may not even be here."

"He'd come back if he wanted a good alibi. He could've slipped away for a few minutes unnoticed, but otherwise all the other actors would say he was here all night."

We dodged around an actor who reached for us.

"There are so many costumes here," I remarked. "Even if the police searched the security footage, it'd be nearly impossible to identify him if he managed to change masks undetected."

We passed a doorway covered by a black curtain. An actor in a red hellish demon mask jumped out from behind it. He was tall, with a strong build. The end of his tattoo sleeve peered out from beneath the red fabric of the cloak he wore.

"I will drag you to the underworld!" the actor hissed with a maniacal laugh.

Fury swept through me because I recognized that voice and tattoo. "Not if I send you there first, you asshole! You're going to tell us everything."

I shoved him as hard as I could, and his back slammed against the wall.

Aster coughed uncontrollably. "What the hell, Elodie? It's all just fun and games!"

Kylan reacted quickly and pinned his strong forearm against Aster's chest. His time in the weight room training for broomball had clearly paid off, because he was an equal match for Luna's ex. He ripped Aster's mask from his face, then tossed it to the floor. "Is that what you call killing your ex?"

Aster went still. "Luna's… dead?"

Kylan's lips curled back in disgust. "I saw a masked man coming out of her room tonight. You wouldn't happen to know anything about that, would you?"

Aster's eyes grew wide. "You think I had anything to do with this?"

"I think things aren't looking great for you, considering the fight you and Luna had last week." Kylan grabbed Aster by the shirt and yanked him toward the curtain. "Let's talk."

I followed them into the classroom. My phone was already in my hand, recording the conversation. If we got a confession, the police would *have* to arrest him.

Kylan shoved Aster into a chair, then withdrew his wand from his pocket and pointed it at our suspect. "Talk."

Aster held his hands up innocently, like he didn't want to cause any trouble. "It's true that Luna and I fought last week, but that was the last time I spoke to her. I certainly didn't kill her!"

I took a step closer. "What was the fight about?"

Aster's hands shook. "I thought she was cheating on me.

She was always spending time with Sam, and I knew something was going on. I'm telling you, that guy is a creep."

My brow furrowed. Luna had never mentioned anyone by that name. "Who's Sam?"

"He's a guy in her Coven History class," Aster explained. "She said they were writing a paper together—some big project that was supposed to be a huge part of their grade. But every time I went to her room, Sam was there, and they said they were *studying*. She's been acting strange and gets all jumpy like she's hiding something. I called her on her bullshit, because I knew she was lying. We got into a screaming match, and we broke up. She said she couldn't be with someone who didn't trust her, and I said I wasn't going to stay if she expected me to blindly buy into her lies."

He sagged against the desk next to him. "I can't believe that's the last thing I'll ever say to her."

Aster looked genuinely devastated, and I knew he wasn't *that* good of an actor.

Kylan must've picked up on it too, because his tone softened. "Can anyone vouch for your whereabouts tonight?"

Aster gestured toward the door. "Ask Logan across the hall. We've been cracking jokes all night. You have to believe that even though I was angry with Luna, I loved her."

Kylan and I exchanged a glance, and I could tell we were both thinking the same thing. Aster didn't do it.

Aster hesitated. "How'd it happen?"

"A curse," I told him. "The police think she accidentally inflicted it upon herself."

Aster shook his head. "She wouldn't."

"If Luna's been acting jumpy lately, maybe it wasn't that she was hiding something from you," Kylan suggested. "Maybe she was scared of someone."

"If you want to know what she was freaked out about, talk to Sam," Aster said. "They've been spending all their time together lately. If she talked to anyone, it was him. He's working the electric chair at Torture Chamber tonight."

Kylan lowered his wand. "You're free to go for now, but know that if you do anything stupid like try to skip town, we'll be back for you."

"I'm staying put, I promise," Aster replied, sounding frightened.

I looked up to Kylan. "On to the Torture Chamber."

CHAPTER 5

We left the Monster's Lair and wove down a few halls until we came upon the entrance to the Torture Chamber. The rattling of chains and participants' screams echoed down the dark hall. We peered into classrooms that were blocked off by ropes. Each one had a different theme, with actors screaming and playing out the torture.

The first room was set up to look like an operating room, with plastic dismembered limbs all around. An actor lay on a table while someone dressed as a doctor pretended to cut into them while they screamed. Fake blood spattered everywhere.

In the next room, a psychic pressed her hand against photo paper, and an inky image formed. "Look!" she cried in a mystical voice. "Look upon your worst fear!"

I averted my gaze before she could show me what fear she saw within me. Thoughtography—or psychic photography—was a technique I'd been learning in my psychic class, in which a clairvoyant could impress their visions upon photo paper. I thought the magic should be used for good, not in this sick, twisted way.

We passed by a room depicting people chained up in a dungeon-like setting, then a shadowed room that played creepy circus music. Terrifying clowns tilted their heads at us, dragging axes behind them. We scurried past them as quickly as we could.

Finally, we came upon a room where a man was strapped to an electric chair. He was thin, with dark hair that fell into his eyes. He certainly looked like the kind of guy who'd hang out in the library with Luna. A strobe light went off, and he screamed and shook in a way that made my stomach twist. If I didn't know this was all fake, it might've nearly convinced me.

Kylan and I stepped over the rope and into the room.

The man in the false electric chair went still. "You're not supposed to do that."

"We aren't here for the haunted house," Kylan said. "We're here to talk to you about Luna Graves. Are you Sam?"

He sat up straighter. "I am. Is everything all right?"

My throat tightened around my words. "Luna was found dead in her dorm room tonight."

Sam's features went stark white. "This is a joke."

"I'm afraid not," I said. "We hear you've been spending a lot of time with her lately. Did she ever mention being afraid of anyone?"

Sam stared at the ground in complete shock. "She never

seemed scared to me, but Luna and I were just essay part-ners. We didn't talk much about our personal lives."

"Her ex-boyfriend seems to think you two were more than just essay partners," Kylan said.

Sam sighed. "I heard about that, but he's wrong. There wasn't anything going on between us. All the time we spent together was spent researching. This project was more than just an essay to her. Luna really thought that we could solve a murder."

The words I'd found in her fireplace came back to me: *Murder in Thornshire*.

"Who's murder were you investigating?" I asked.

"We weren't sure it *was* murder, but Luna never believed that the kid who died at the Enchanted Ball jumped from the balcony. So when we were assigned this paper to write about a significant event in the coven's history, Luna pushed for us to write about the suicide. She thought with enough research, we could prove there was more to the death of Emerson Hawthorne."

The corners of my vision blurred. I stumbled to the side, nearly losing my place in the room as the strobe light continued flashing. Kylan caught me, his strong arms drag-ging me upright.

"W—why didn't she tell me?" I rasped.

Sam eyed me curiously. "You're Luna's cousin, aren't you? You look like her."

I nodded, struggling to find any words.

"She talked about you when we discussed interviewing witnesses," Sam admitted. "But she didn't want you to know she was working on this. She thought it'd hurt too much to bring it up."

She wasn't wrong. I'd barely talked about Emerson since the day we gave him a proper witch's burial—a shallow grave without a casket, meant to bring his body back to nature soon after death. I couldn't think about him without seeing the odd twist of his neck, his body sprawled out on the concrete three stories below me.

"What makes her think it wasn't a suicide?" I dared to ask.

Sam hesitated, then gave a heavy sigh. "She did a séance after Emerson's death. She saw how much you were struggling and thought that contacting him would give you the chance to say goodbye."

My jaw hung slack. "She talked to his spirit? Every time we tried, we couldn't get through to him."

"She *barely* did," Sam said. "From what she told me, Emerson's ghost claimed he didn't jump."

My hand curled tightly around Kylan's wrist, just to keep myself upright.

"If she didn't think he killed himself, what *does* she think happened?" Kylan asked. "Emerson was alone on the balcony that night."

"That's what we were trying to piece together with our essay," Sam replied.

"Do you have a copy of this essay?" I asked. I *had* to know what Luna had learned.

"I have a hard copy of one of our early drafts, but Luna's got the latest copy on her computer. Last I saw her, she was headed back to her dorm to work on the paper. We obtained important information at the cemetery today that changes everything. I had to get to Haunted Halls because I was scheduled to work, but Luna offered to organize our research, so we went our separate ways."

"What kind of information?" Kylan asked.

"We visited Emerson's gravesite to do a spell Luna's been researching for weeks that would reveal the cause of death. It was a potent spell—something that could only be done on Halloween and performed over his bones. We learned that it wasn't the fall that killed him. Emerson had some sort of potion in his system at the time of death."

A lump rose to my throat.

Kylan's eyebrows pinched together. "Didn't the police do a spell to determine the cause of death at the scene?"

Sam nodded. "Yes, but after contacting his ghost, Luna was convinced they missed something."

"So, the potion killed him?" I asked.

"We aren't sure, entirely," Sam confessed. "All we know is this proves there's more to the case than what the police reports showed. It looked like a suicide, so no one investigated further. If that got overlooked, what else did?"

My fingers shook against Kylan's arm. "Emerson snagged a vial off a police officer that night. We thought it was alcohol, but it could've been a potion."

Kylan's eyes shifted in a calculating manner. "It's possible it's connected. But this tells us nothing about the guy in the hockey mask I saw leaving Luna's room."

Sam's eyes widened even more, though I didn't think that was possible. "You asked if Luna was afraid of someone. You think she was *killed*?"

"We're looking into that possibility," Kylan admitted. "Did Luna ever mention anyone she trusted, someone she might've talked to if someone was following her?"

Sam thought about it for a moment. "She never said anything to me, but she might've talked to Professor Wilde. She's our Coven History professor, but she's also Luna's academic advisor. She's working the Death Cemetery in the cafeteria tonight."

"Thank you for all your help, Sam." I turned to leave, but Sam stopped me.

"Elodie?" Tears of sadness welled in Sam's eyes. "I'm sorry about your cousin… and your friend."

The kind gesture was enough to make me break down. The strobe light went off again, and inexplicable panic rose within me. I couldn't take it anymore. I ran out of the room, sprinting down hallways to get far away—from what, I wasn't sure.

I heard Kylan's footsteps following me, but I couldn't bring myself to slow down. I turned a few corners and ducked behind one of the curtains separating the hallways. I staggered to the side, catching myself against an old painting. A sharp corner of the frame sliced my hand, and I felt the warmth of blood pooling in my palm. I hardly noticed the pain past my panic.

I leaned against the wall as the memories of that night came rushing back.

CHAPTER 6

Kylan spun me around the dancefloor, and my purple ballgown swirled around my ankles. I'd been looking forward to the Enchanted Ball all year. It was our last big celebration before high school graduation, and I felt like a princess in the arms of the man I loved.

People always said Kylan and I would last long after high school ended, and I believed it with my entire being. We had our entire future planned out. We would study alongside one another at the academy, get married during graduate school, then buy a house on the lake after graduation. There was a cluster of cute cottages up the road from the estate where the ball was being held, and we both agreed that'd be the perfect place to raise a family. At eighteen, we were still young to be making these plans, but we both knew what we wanted out of our future. Kylan planned to become a potions master teaching at the college, and I would pursue psychic studies to become an Intuit. It's what all the best psychics in the coven did.

We were already starting to come into our powers. Every day, our abilities to cast protection charms and banishing spells grew stronger. I'd started having visions in my dreams, and Kylan was already brewing healing salves. My best friend Katie and her boyfriend Riley were both adept at divination through the use of palmology, tarot reading, and carromancy. Our friend Emerson had taken an interest in enchanting.

I glanced around the ballroom, taking in the immense beauty of the night. The Enchanted Ball was hosted on the top floor of the largest cranberry farm in the area. The mansion was fairly new, but the farm had been operating for years. Now, the place hosted weddings and other events throughout the year.

They'd really gone all out for the Enchanted Ball. The ceiling had been enchanted to look like the night sky, with illusions of stars twinkling overhead. Beneath the illusion hovered witch balls—hollow glass spheres in all different colors used for warding off evil spirits. Each glass ball seemed to catch the light of the twinkling stars to project their sparkle across the dancefloor.

On stage, a band of undead skeletons enchanted by necromancy magic played a slow song with a haunting tune. A buffet of enchanted sweets lined one wall, with all kinds of tarts and cakes that made you blow heart bubbles or turned your hair funny colors when you ate them. The opposite wall housed floor-to-ceiling windows that looked out over the cranberry fields, and double doors that led onto a balcony stood propped open.

Riley spun Katie around from beside us, and the sound of my friends' laughter filled the air. I didn't want this night to end, because being here in this magical place surrounded by the people I loved felt like I'd found the glory of the afterlife right here.

Except Emerson was still missing. He said he'd be here, so I didn't know what was taking him so long.

"Have you seen Emerson yet?" I shouted to Kylan over the music.

He shook his head. "I'm sure he'll be here soon. He wouldn't miss this!"

Kylan wrapped a hand around my waist and dragged me closer to him. I inhaled his sandalwood scent, and my heart lifted until I felt like I was floating.

The second my body pressed into his, something changed. The sparkling lights in the room seemed to dim, and the music faded like I was hearing it from underwater. A tingling sensation spread down my arms, and bile rose to my throat.

I stiffened, but a moment later my senses were back. I frantically glanced around the room, but everyone kept on smiling and dancing. It seemed I was the only one who noticed the strange shift in the air.

Kylan leaned down to press a kiss to my cheek, but I barely noticed what was happening before he was already drawing away. His features fell. "Everything alright, Elle? You look like you've seen a ghost."

"Not a ghost," I told him. "But I felt something. I can't explain it, but I have a really bad feeling."

Kylan immediately took my hand and started leading me off the dancefloor. "Let's sit down."

Katie and Riley noticed our abrupt exit and rushed to follow us.

"Is everything all right?" Katie helped me sit down at our table, looking concerned.

"I'm fine," I said. "I just feel… weird."

"Weird, like some sort of vision?" Riley asked.

I shook my head. "No, this is different."

So far, my visions had only been little things like predicting the cafeteria lunch menu. I'd never felt anything quite as strange as this. My whole body buzzed with an energy that kept me alert and glancing around the ball-room, but everyone was laughing and having a good time.

"I'll get you some water." Kylan hurried off, then came back from the buffet table a few moments later with bottled water.

I sipped the drink and found my unease settling. "I guess it's just dehydration."

"Heeey!" someone called happily, stealing our attention. "Why the long faces? Let's get this party started!"

We all turned to see Emerson dancing up to our table. He looked out of breath. His curls were a mess atop his head, but he wore a bright pink suit that looked surprisingly good on him. Emerson never was one to downplay flair. He loved being the center of attention. I think it distracted him from how he felt most days. He never really talked about it, but I knew his home life wasn't good. We all took turns having him over for dinner, partly to make sure he was getting enough to eat, and partly to give him an excuse to avoid home.

I shook off the strange feeling as I got to my feet to pull my friend into a hug. "Emerson! It's not a party without you. You better have a good excuse for being late."

Emerson smirked. "Boy, do I have a story for you."

"How about you tell it on the balcony, where we can hear?" Kylan shouted over the music.

The five of us stepped onto the empty balcony. I shivered in the cool air. Out here, the music was still loud, but we could hear each other better.

Emerson launched into a dramatic retelling of the night's events. "You know how my mom's car has been rattling for the last week? Well, I went to turn it on, and the damn thing wouldn't start! So I figured I'd travel the old-fashioned way. I enchanted a broom to fly across town, but the cops picked me up halfway here. They claimed this magic was too advanced for a kid who hasn't enrolled in the academy yet. They wanted to charge me with unauthorized spellcasting."

"You seriously enchanted a broom!?" Riley balked. "That's a second-year spell, and we're only coming into our powers. You know what overloading your system can do."

Emerson shrugged. "Relax. I'm still here, aren't I? It's not like the enchantment was hard."

I always knew Emerson was really talented, and I had no doubt he would excel in his courses once he got out of his parents' house. The fact that he could pull off an enchanting spell without proper training proved that.

"Obviously, they didn't arrest you or you'd be sitting in a jail cell," I said. "They didn't press charges?"

"Nah, I feigned ignorance and talked them down to a ticket," Emerson said proudly. "They let me go, and I walked the rest of the way."

"You should've called us," Katie insisted.

"Yeah, we would've come to pick you up," Kylan agreed.

Emerson shrugged. "I didn't want to bother you."

It was no inconvenience at all to drive across town to get him, so I knew there must be more going on. I bet his mom didn't pay the phone bill again.

"Besides, it wasn't all bad." Emerson shot a glance to the doors, then turned toward the banister as he reached into his suitcoat. "I figured if I was going to pay a fine, I should get something in return."

Emerson withdrew a glass vial from his pocket. It was wide and skinny, like a flask. A dark maroon liquid that looked like red wine sloshed inside of it.

Kylan eyed the flask warily. "What is that?"

Emerson's smirk grew wider. "Alcohol, I would think. Saw it sitting in the officer's cup holder when he pinned me against the side of his cruiser. Someone's been drinking on the job."

"And instead of reporting it, you stole it?" I demanded. It didn't surprise me that Emerson would steal alcohol, but to steal it from a police officer was definitely a new one.

"I deserved my money's worth!" Emerson popped the cork off the top and held the vial outward. "Anyone?"

We all shared a wary glance and shook our heads.

"We should get rid of it before—" Kylan started to say,

but Emerson had already brought the vial to his lips and took a swig.

"Whew!" Emerson shook his head and made a sour face. "That's stronger than my mom's whiskey."

"Emerson, please stop." I knew he wanted to have a good time, but this was nothing but bad news. He wasn't even trying to hide it, and if he got caught he'd be in huge trouble.

He ignored me and brought the vial back to his lips. He downed another gulp. "Look, if you don't want to have a good time, that's on you."

"We can have a good time inside," I pressed. "Come dance with us. It'll be fun! Like old times, when we all used to dance around the bonfire at the lake."

"Old times?" Emerson sneered. "You mean before my dad got caught conning the town with his fake potions? Dancing isn't going to make me feel better, Elle."

Kylan's features grew visibly tense. "Put the vial away, Emerson."

"Or what?" Emerson demanded. "You'll get rid of it for me?"

"Em, come on," Riley insisted. "We all just want to have a good time."

Emerson scowled. "But you're going to dictate how I do it? You're all judging me. I can see it on your faces. So if you all want to dance, go dance. I'll be out here having my own good time."

Emerson turned away from us, leaning against the balcony as he stared over the cranberry fields. His defensiveness wasn't unusual. It was his way of asking us for space when he couldn't communicate that directly. I figured more had happened tonight than he was telling us. I wouldn't be surprised if he got into a fight with his mom over the car, then enchanted the broom to get away from her.

Emerson wasn't always forthcoming about what was going on at home, and we all knew better than to pry. We'd all learned that the best thing to do was give him a few minutes to compose himself, then distract him with something less serious.

"All right," Katie said lightly. "We'll be inside if you decide you want to dance."

My friends turned toward the double doors, but I lingered for a moment. The strange sensation in my gut returned.

"Are you going to be okay, Em?" I asked softly.

He didn't turn back to me. "I'm just doing the best I can, Elle. I'll be inside in a few."

I left him on the balcony and found Kylan waiting for me just inside the doors.

"He'll be fine," Kylan said. "He just needs a moment."

Kylan led me onto the dancefloor, and though I spun around in his arms, I kept shooting glances toward the balcony. Emerson looked hopeless leaning against the banister, his head hung low. I thought he might be crying, but if Emerson had one rule, it was to never let anyone see him cry.

I spun around again, before my gaze drifted back to the windows to find the balcony empty. A nauseating sickness slammed into my gut, and I clutched my stomach right there on the dancefloor. My eyes darted from one side of the room to the other.

"Where'd Emerson go!?" I shouted. A terrifying feeling that I couldn't explain rose within me. Before anyone could answer, I was racing across the dancefloor. I hurried onto the balcony, thinking Emerson must be hiding somewhere in the shadows, but he was gone. I didn't understand. I'd only just seen him a second ago. He couldn't have gone far.

Slowly, I inched forward, my heels clicking ominously against the stone as I approached the banister. I peered over the ledge…

And let out an earth-shattering scream.

Three stories below me, my friend lay sprawled out on the concrete, his neck twisted at an odd angle and a pool of blood growing beneath him.

Kylan raced onto the balcony and pulled me away from the banister.

Tears streamed down my cheeks as my body rocked with sobs. "He's gone!"

I was vaguely aware of several other people coming onto the balcony, but I couldn't process how many. Katie put her hand on my shoulder, but even the usual comfort of my best friend's touch couldn't soothe me now.

I couldn't make any sense of what had happened. Emerson was a lot of things, but he wasn't a bad friend. He'd lie to his parents, his teachers, or the police, but he'd never lied to me. He promised he'd be inside in a few minutes.

Emerson never broke a promise.

CHAPTER 7

The memories of that night faded as the school hallway came back into focus. Kylan stood in front of me, his hands on my shoulders to steady me. My back was still pressed against the wall, and my palm stung from where I'd sliced it on the picture frame. I looked around to find we were standing in a quiet, empty hallway far away from the haunted house. The door to an alchemy lab stood open across from us, where potion vials lining the shelves glowed in all different colors. Otherwise, the hall was illuminated only by the soft glow of the moonlight shining in through a row of windows.

"Are you with me?" Kylan asked gently.

I nodded, but my tone cracked. "I can't get that night out of my head. I'll always wonder what would've happened if I stayed on that balcony with him. Maybe he'd still be here."

"You couldn't have known what would happen, Elle."

"But I did, in a way," I countered. "I had a really bad feeling that night. I should've listened to it."

"I'm not saying you're wrong about your psychic feeling, but you couldn't have known what it meant. No one blames you."

I yanked away from him, my tone turning bitter. "Katie and Riley do."

"Katie and Riley don't matter. If you ask me, they were real jerks after what happened on graduation night, and frankly I don't think you should be around shitty friends like them."

I frowned when he brought up graduation. That night, the four of us were supposed to go out to the woods and dig up a memory box we placed there when we were kids. We'd been planning it since middle school, ever since we snuck out there the first night we witnessed Emerson's bruises. We'd been trying to cheer him up, and we buried the memory box as a promise to stay friends until the end.

The end had come far too soon. After Emerson died, we agreed to dig up the box like we planned, only we were going to place a memorial for him in its place. We held our own private memorial service and threw petals into the river for him, then drove to the woods to say our final goodbyes.

That night, I got that same terrible feeling again, only I couldn't get the image of my mother's face out of my mind. I couldn't let something bad happen to her the way it happened to Emerson, so I ditched my friends and took the car we'd all driven to the woods with.

When I got home, my mom was perfectly fine. I stayed

with her for hours, just to make sure. Nothing bad happened.

Katie and Riley were pissed I'd ditch such an important night for *some stupid feeling that meant nothing*, as they put it. They never really forgave me for leaving them out in the woods all night.

"I don't blame Katie and Riley," I said. "I gave up our special night we'd planned for years, and an important tribute to Emerson, all because of an upset stomach."

Kylan frowned. "I never believed that."

Blood dripped from my palm then. Kylan's gaze immediately fell to the splatter on the tile, which was surprisingly bright red in the dim moonlight.

His eyes widened in concern. "You're hurt."

I curled my hand into a fist. "It's just a scratch."

Kylan reached for my wrist to turn my palm over, and my skin heated where he touched me. "It's more than a scratch. I know a good healing potion we can brew. Let me help you."

Before I could respond, Kylan dragged me into the alchemy lab. A cauldron sat on a table in the center of the room. He pulled up a chair for me, then found a clean towel that I pressed to my palm. The glowing potions stacked on shelves around the room illuminated his workstation.

Kylan began shuffling through drawers to gather supplies. "I know you think you overreacted on graduation night, but we can't know what would've happened if you didn't get to your mom that night. She could've gotten into her car and been in a bad accident, or slipped getting out of the tub. But none of that happened because you were there. For all we know, your feeling changed the future."

I eyed him as he poured herbs and strange-colored liquids into the cauldron. He didn't have to measure the ingredients; he was a natural. "I've only been having visions for a few months, and I barely know how to interpret them. I don't know how you can have so much faith in me."

"Because I *know* you, Elodie." Kylan found a wooden spoon and began mixing the potion. While he stirred, tendrils of mesmerizing teal magic swirled down his arm and settled into the cauldron. "You're someone who considers every angle before coming to a conclusion. If you think something bad is going to happen, then I think you're right. Tonight proves that, because you got that same feeling again walking to Luna's dorm. If that's not enough to prove that you saved your mom on graduation night, then I don't know what is."

I hesitated. "I guess I'll never know for sure."

Kylan spooned the potion into an empty vial, then knelt in front of me. "If this is too much for you, we'll stop. We can hand over our recordings to the police and let them piece everything together."

I shook my head. "I don't want to do that. The police brushed off that paper I found in her fireplace. I think it might've been her essay, and if they aren't going to take that seriously, then they won't care about the rest of this. I want to keep going."

Kylan held the vial out to me. Its contents shimmered

and glowed white. "Then let's get you all fixed up and continue on."

Our skin brushed as I took the vial from him. I did my best to steady my trembling fingers as I brought the bottle to my lips. The potion was sweet, with a slight hint of cranberry. The pain throbbing through my palm ebbed away. Gently, Kylan took my injured hand and removed the towel. The wound had vanished, like it hadn't been there at all.

He wiped away the rest of the blood, then flashed a kind smile. "Good as new."

My pulse quickened as his fingers lingered on mine. "Thank you."

Our eyes locked for longer than I cared to admit. Kylan cleared his throat, then started fumbling to return his supplies back where he found them. "We should get going."

We started down the hall, but I quickly realized we didn't know where we were going. We didn't have any classes in this part of the building, and everything looked different in the dark. "I'm not sure which way's out."

"I'm sure something around here is familiar." Kylan stopped in front of a painting depicting a black cat beside a cauldron. "I recognize this painting. We can't be too far from the entry hall."

I ran my fingers over the edge of the frame. It reminded me of the warmth of Kylan's kisses. "We kissed in front of this painting during our campus tour senior year."

"I remember." Kylan's tone didn't give anything away. "It seems like a lifetime ago."

"It was," I replied softly.

I remembered that day so clearly. Kylan and I had snuck off from our tour group during lunch and met in a secluded hallway.

"One day, we'll kiss in every room at this academy," Kylan had promised in a sultry tone.

"Why not get started right now?" I remembered teasing. I'd taken a step toward him, until his back was pressed against a doorway. I ran my hands over his chest, then down his arms. *"No one's around, and we have a few minutes before they'll notice us missing."*

I'd lifted myself on my toes to place a passionate kiss on his lips.

I still remembered the way his eyes closed to drink me in. *"Keep kissing me like that, and we're going to get in trouble. We'll be caught."*

"Then why don't we go someplace more private?" I'd encouraged.

I recalled the coolness of the doorknob as I twisted the handle behind him. His lips were on mine before we fully entered the room. It'd been a classroom for psychics, with big plush couches circling tables set with crystal balls. Kylan and I had fallen onto one of the couches, and he'd grabbed my ass to pull me onto his lap.

"Kiss me everywhere," I remembered begging him.

And he did. More than once.

I quickly shrugged off the memory, bringing myself back to the present.

"I wish I understood why that life together had to end," Kylan said gently. "If it was because being with me reminded you too much of our friends, I'd have done everything to help you forget your past. I'd have changed my name and taken a potion to change my face… whatever would've made it easier for you, as long as we were together in the end."

I started walking down the hall. "It's not that, and you already know it. I told you I had a bad feeling about us. I wasn't going to risk another bad feeling again."

"If that's what helps you sleep at night, you can keep on believing that, but I know you well enough to know when you're lying, even to yourself. If you really trusted your gut, you wouldn't have brushed your bad feeling off earlier tonight."

I whirled on him. "Don't you *dare* blame me for what happened to Luna!"

Kylan scowled. "That's the last thing I would *ever* do, Elle. All I'm saying is that what happened between us has nothing to do with your psychic abilities. You want to know what I really think? I think you're scared of how close we were. You're afraid that if you love me too hard, you can lose me, and that it will hurt more than anything. You're trying to protect yourself from this pain, but I need you to understand that *I* will protect you, Elle."

Then Kylan *got down on his knees.*

I stepped back. "Please get up."

"I'm not getting up until I tell you how I really feel, and I need you to hear it, Elle. Losing Emerson was hell, but watching your grief consume you in the aftermath has been excruciating. I wish you knew that every time you cry, I long to wipe away your tears. Every moment you feel like you're falling apart, I yearn to be there holding you together."

He inched closer to me, and I didn't stop him when he reached out to take my hand. "If you don't want me here, then that's fine, but I'm not letting you go until I know you're not lying to yourself anymore. I want you, Elle, and nothing we have gone through, and nothing we will ever go through, will ever change that. If it takes the rest of our lives to convince you of that, I'll do it, because you're worth waiting a thousand lifetimes for. I know you were afraid after everything that happened. It's okay to be scared, but it doesn't have to stop you. Can we try again?"

Tears welled in my eyes. Being with him had been heaven on earth, but that time in our lives was over now. Everything he promised me was too good to be true, because we'd already been there. He'd *tried*. He'd held me and wiped my tears, and none of it was enough.

It never would be.

I took another step back, my fingers falling out of his. "I'm sorry, Kylan. I can't."

His face was too shadowed for me to witness his reaction, but I knew it couldn't be anything less than heartbreaking. He cleared his throat and stood. "If you ever change your mind, I'm right here."

I turned my back to him. "It doesn't matter. Right now, all that matters is finding out what happened to Luna. Let's get moving."

CHAPTER 8

We wove through a maze of hallways, until we reached the cafeteria. A wooden sign had words scratched into it.

Beware those who enter here
For all cemetery dwellers die
Find the key meant only for the living
To get to the other side

Kylan cocked an eyebrow. "The other side, huh? A very clever double meaning."

We entered the cafeteria, and the doors clicked shut behind us. Inside the room, tables had been moved out of the way and replaced by fake headstones. Fog rolled across the ground, and skeletons enchanted with necromancy magic rose out of coffins. Students dressed as zombies moaned as they limped around the fake graveyard. Two real ghosts floated around the perimeter of the room.

The illusion of a tree stood near the center of the cafeteria, and a fake car made from foam and cardboard looked like it'd smashed into it. A guy covered in fake blood lay on the hood of the smashed car, really driving home the riddle about how all cemetery dwellers die here.

On the opposite end of the room was a double doorway covered in a fake chain and a big padlock. Other ticket holders roamed the room, looking for the key to get out.

A zombie actor lunged for us, but I didn't play along. Instead, I asked him, "Is Professor Wilde here?"

The actor pointed toward the illusion of the big tree. Behind it in the shadows, I caught the motion of someone swirling their arms. A breeze swept through the room, though there were no open windows. Fog swirled around our ankles, and a group of girls next to us squealed.

Kylan and I headed to where the actor had pointed. There, we found a woman in a black dress with long, silver hair flowing over her shoulders waving a wand around. The fog and illusion of tree branches responded to her commands.

"Professor Wilde?" I asked.

"Yes, dear. Can I help you?" She continued waving her wand.

"We'd like to talk to you about Luna Graves. I'm her cousin," I said.

Professor Wilde froze, her wand still lifted. "Luna sent you?"

Kylan shook his head. "We're afraid not. Luna was found dead in her dorm room earlier tonight."

Professor Wilde dropped her wand, and it rolled across

the ground at our feet. "No... I just saw her a few hours ago."

"You spoke with her tonight?" Kylan prodded.

Professor Wilde fumbled with the layers on her dress and pulled her phone from her pocket. "I was worried about her. Luna sent me this."

She showed us a message on her phone that read, *If you don't hear from me in an hour, I'm at 613 Proctor Way.*

I felt all the blood drain from my face. Luna was definitely scared of something... or someone.

"My number's listed on my faculty page in case of emergencies, so I didn't realize it was her at first," Professor Wilde said. "I called the number, and I got worried when I heard Luna answer. She insisted she was fine and was just working on her essay for my class. I told her not to worry about it because it was Halloween and she should be celebrating. When I asked her about the message, she said it was just a precaution, that it was best to share her location with someone she trusted."

Usually, she'd share that information with me, but Sam had been clear Luna didn't want me knowing about this paper.

"That's the last you heard from her?" I wondered.

Professor Wilde shook her head. "She came here to talk to me about an hour after she sent that message. She showed up here frazzled, insisting that she couldn't continue with her essay. When I pressed her for details, she said she couldn't talk about it."

Her gaze grew distant, like she couldn't believe what happened. "I managed to calm her down. We agreed that she would turn in all her materials on my desk in the morning, and from there we'd reassess her project. In the meantime, I walked her back to her dorm room, and that was the last time I saw her."

Professor Wilde shuddered, looking disturbed. She threw her hand over her mouth, and I thought she was going to puke. "Excuse me for a moment."

Professor Wilde rushed off, and though she expected us to stay there to chat longer, I'd heard enough.

I turned to Kylan. "Luna was here earlier tonight, which means the ticket I found was *hers*, not the killer's. We have to go to that address she sent to Professor Wilde. Whatever happened there shook Luna up."

Kylan was already on the move. "Let's go."

As we turned around, I realized we didn't have a clear exit. The ghosts had hovered over to the door we'd come through, and the other doors were covered in chains.

Kylan sighed. "We don't have time for games."

I tapped my chin, thinking of the riddle we'd seen on our way in. "This shouldn't be too hard. I bet it's a play on words. A key could mean anything—a key in music, maybe a cypher or code of some sort. Though this car wreck looks very suspicious... Dead people don't need cars, so maybe the key meant for the living is a car key?"

We approached the fake car, which had the driver's side door ripped off. A seat from a real car had been positioned inside. I ducked my head in and sat in the driver's seat.

"I don't see a key, but there's a laptop here," Kylan pointed out. The laptop had been propped up near the driver, like in a police car.

I noticed that the *Enter* key had been painted red. "I think we found our *key*."

"I get it! Beware those who *Enter* here," Kylan said.

I clicked the *Enter* button, and the doors ahead of us swung open.

Kylan smirked. "What was that you were saying about us not being able to work together?"

"All right," I caved. "We make a good team."

Kylan quickly helped me out of the car, and we rushed out of the cafeteria.

I didn't know what we'd find at 613 Proctor Way, but I hoped it was enough to bring my cousin's killer to justice.

CHAPTER 9

The fastest way across town was on brooms. Once we were outside Haunted Halls, Kylan spoke an incantation to summon two brooms from the broomball field. They came flying out of the darkness, straight into our outstretched palms. We quickly mounted the brooms and took to the skies. Dark clouds swirled above us, and the wind bit at my cheeks as we flew over peaked roofs and the tall turrets of Victorian homes.

We landed on a quiet, secluded street in a nice part of town. It was nearing the witching hour, and everyone was at their parties or rituals at this time of night. The houses here were all three stories, with big yards and wraparound porches.

We left our brooms leaning against a thick oak tree and approached the house Luna had spoken of. Although orange and purple lights lit up the yard, the inside of the house was dark. I pulled my wand from my bag, then hit *record* on my phone.

Before I could step on the lawn, Kylan grabbed my elbow. He pointed toward the house and kept his voice low. "There's a security camera on the front porch."

"Let's go around back," I whispered.

We slunk through the darkness. I shot wary glances around the backyard, but we were completely alone. A set of sliding glass doors led onto a patio, but I didn't see any security cameras here.

I crept behind Kylan toward the door. "How are we going to get in? We don't know who lives here or what security measures they have in place. If we break a window, it could trigger an alarm."

Kylan reached for the door handle, and to my surprise, the door slid open easily. "Looks like we don't have to break anything."

I thought it was strange that the owners had a security camera out front but hadn't bothered locking their back door. I figured they must've forgotten in the midst of the Halloween festivities.

We crept inside to find ourselves in a large kitchen. I glanced around for clues as to who lived here, but it was hard to see much of anything in the darkness. All I could really make out was a wooden door with a swirling star design carved in the center. Then my gaze landed on the kitchen table, where a hockey stick lay beside a sports duffel bag.

A noise down the hall startled us both. It sounded like shuffling papers.

Kylan placed an index finger to his lips, then carefully

reached for the hockey stick. He held it over his shoulder like a baseball bat as he inched down the hall. My heart hammered as I followed behind him.

An ominous orange glow appeared through a doorway ahead of us. We were near the front of the house now, and I could only assume the room we approached was the living room. Slowly, we peered around the corner.

My entire body gave a start when I realized we weren't alone. A figure crouched at the hearth, holding a stack of papers over tall flames. I guess now we knew why the back door was unlocked. The fire cast shadows across the man's face. I recognized that dark hair and wide eyes.

"Sam?" I demanded.

Luna's essay partner jumped. Sam shot to his feet and held the papers toward the flames in a threatening way. "Don't come any closer! I'll burn the essay, and you'll never know what happened to your friend."

I realized the stack of papers was the essay draft Sam had mentioned in the Torture Chamber. Luna's draft had been burned, too. The pieces began to fall together in my mind.

"It was *you*," Kylan sneered. "You killed Luna."

Sam trembled. "If you think I'm going to talk, you're wrong. What are you doing here? You shouldn't be able to get into the house past my father's wards."

"His wards must not be very strong," Kylan replied. "Give it up, Sam. You've been caught."

"You don't know anything!" Sam shouted.

I stepped out from behind Kylan, fuming. "We know

Luna was here earlier tonight. You said the last time you saw her was at the cemetery, when you did that spell to determine Emerson's cause of death. But the two of you came back here to work on your paper together. Luna was scared enough to message Professor Wilde her location. Aster said she'd been acting jumpy, like she was afraid of someone. It was *you*. After she left your house, she told Professor Wilde she had to withdraw from the project. What did you do to her?"

"I—I..." Sam seemed wholly shocked that we'd put the pieces together. "I didn't touch her, if that's what you're thinking. I was just angry. I didn't know Luna messaged Professor Wilde, or I never would've sent you to talk to her. I just needed to get rid of you."

"So you could come back and burn your essay, just like you did with the copy in Luna's dorm?" I demanded. "What's so important about that essay that you have to get rid of it?"

"It... reminds me of her," Sam admitted. "I wanted to be with her, but she turned me down."

Kylan scoffed. "Aster was right. You *are* a creep."

I wanted nothing more than to cast the same curse that killed Luna, to show Sam how she suffered. But I'd never stoop that low. I had to get a clear confession out of him, then I could turn my recording over to the police and they would administer his sentencing.

"Let me get this straight," I snarled. "You spent the day with Luna working on your project, and the moment you get her alone in your house, you come on to her. But your sorry ass couldn't handle the rejection."

I was so angry that I took a step forward, ready to punch him across the jaw.

"I said don't come any closer!" Sam thrust the essay into the fire, and the flames roared as they consumed the paper.

I hardly cared about the essay right now. "You followed her back to her dorm, when you could conceal yourself and get away unnoticed. Everyone was going to be in costume, and the Haunted Halls would give you an alibi. Luna cast that curse to defend herself because she was terrified of *you*!"

Tears streaked Sam's cheeks. He was a complete blubbering mess and looked absolutely pathetic. "Yes! All right, I killed her! Is that what you want to hear?"

"I don't care if that curse came out of Luna's wand or not, because it's still your fault," I sneered. "You're the one responsible. You killed Luna Graves."

Sam lifted his hand, and a powerful spell sizzling around the edges burst out of his palm. I ducked, but Kylan jumped in front of me. The spell slammed into Kylan's chest, and he was knocked off his feet. He landed with a heavy *oof* on the couch, and the hockey stick clattered to the ground.

Kylan recovered quickly and leapt to his feet, pulling out his wand. "You leave Elodie alone!"

The light flicked on, and I was shocked to see a tall man standing in a doorway on the opposite end of the room. A sheriff's badge glinted from his uniform. I didn't know how the sheriff had found us, but the fear rising in my chest subsided. Thank our lucky stars the police were here.

Sam whirled around. "Dad?"

Kylan lowered his wand. "Your dad's the sheriff?"

Sheriff Woodfield's eyes landed on Kylan and me. "What's going on here?"

Sam wiped his eyes. "They know, Dad. They know I killed Luna."

Sheriff Woodfield's face paled, like he couldn't believe his son could be involved in something like this. "Luna's death was an accident."

Sam swallowed hard, then leveled his father with a dark stare. "You know the truth, Dad. We both do. I killed her. I was standing in that room when she cast the curse."

I pulled my phone from my pocket. "We have recordings of the full story, Sheriff, including testimony from other witnesses."

Sheriff Woodfield's jaw hung slack as the weight of his son's confession hit him. I could see the moment he realized that he had to arrest his own son. He quickly composed himself.

"I regret to do this, Sam, but I can't ignore your confession." Sheriff Woodfield withdrew his wand and aimed it at his son. Magic swirled around Sam's arms, binding his wrists behind his back. "Samuel Woodfield, you are under arrest for the murder of Luna Graves."

The sheriff did his best to conceal his emotions as he marched forward to do his job. He grabbed Sam's arm and led him outside to the police cruiser. Kylan and I followed.

Sheriff Woodfield slammed the back door behind Sam, then turned to us. "You were right, Miss Graves. There was more to the case, and I apologize that I didn't listen closer."

"You were just looking at the evidence in front of you," I

replied. "You didn't know Luna, but I did, and I knew something else must be going on."

"We'll have to admit everything you found into evidence," the sheriff said.

I nodded. "I understand."

The sheriff took my phone. I didn't care to give it up, as long as it got Sam convicted.

Sheriff Woodfield shifted his weight between his feet. "Sam was burning something in the fireplace when I got home. Do you know what it was?"

"It was his essay that he'd been writing with Luna," Kylan answered. "They were investigating Emerson Hawthorne's death."

The sheriff appeared curious. "Were there any other copies that you know of?"

"Luna had a copy, but Sam burned it in her dorm when he was there earlier tonight," I said. "Otherwise, he said the only other copy was on her computer."

The sheriff nodded. "Thank you for your cooperation in this matter. The witching hour has passed, and it's getting late. The two of you should get back to campus. I'll be in touch if we need anything further."

Then the sheriff climbed into the cruiser and turned the lights on. He stole a glance in the review mirror and spoke to Sam. I couldn't be sure of what he said, but I thought I heard, "I'll get you out of this, son."

I turned to Kylan once the sheriff pulled out of the driveway. "They're going to go easy on him because he's the sheriff's son."

"That doesn't change what we did here tonight," Kylan

insisted. "Your intuition told you there was more going on, and we followed that nudge to uncover the truth. Regardless of Sam's conviction, shouldn't that count for something?"

"It should," I agreed.

Only, it didn't feel like enough.

CHAPTER 10

I was exhausted by the time we returned to campus. Kylan walked me back to my dorm and paused outside my room. I didn't want him to go, but I knew it wasn't a good idea to invite him inside. His mere proximity made me want to crawl into his arms, where I knew I'd be safe enough to sleep soundlessly. We were both vulnerable enough tonight to let it happen.

But I couldn't.

I paused with my hand on the door handle. "I wish I could just forget everything that happened."

Kylan frowned. "You know the coven doesn't have any spells that can do that."

It was a shame, because if we did, I'd have considered it long ago.

"Are you going to be okay on your own?" he asked.

"I'll be all right," I lied. "Goodnight."

I left Kylan in the hall and collapsed into bed. It was a restless sleep. My dreams replayed the night over and over, until the dreams became so sick and twisted that all I could see were Luna's and Emerson's bodies lying next to one another in a shallow grave. Flesh rotted from their bones, and maggots wiggled through their eye sockets.

I woke with a start the following morning. My dreams left me feeling uneasy, and all I wanted was to wash the previous night off of me. My feet felt like cinderblocks as I dragged myself to the shower. I barely noticed the hot water searing my skin, as my mind was completely elsewhere. I thought solving Luna's death would make me feel better, but now I didn't know what to feel at all.

The grief was all-consuming, and on top of that, I was confused about where I stood with Kylan. I'd been avoiding him so long that I forgot how good it felt to be in his presence. Last night was a reminder of everything we once shared. I didn't think we could ever get that back, and it felt like I was going to have to let go of it all over again.

The hot water did nothing to curb my unease. I couldn't stop thinking about Emerson, and how Luna had learned that he didn't die from the fall. We may have caught Luna's killer, but Emerson's story deserved to be put to rest, too.

I got dressed and twisted my hair into a bun. I hurried into the hall… and stopped in my tracks. Kylan lay in front of my door. He wore a fresh t-shirt and had gotten rid of his wolf hat and gloves, but it looked like he'd slept in the hall all night. Kylan stirred.

"What are you doing here?" I asked.

He pushed himself upright. "I had to make sure you were safe."

I didn't know what to make of that, but I managed to stammer out a response. "I—I'm all right."

He looked me up and down. "Are you sure?"

I hated how well he could read me. "All right, I'm not fine. Luna was investigating Emerson's death, and she learned he had a potion in his system when he died. I have to know what really happened. I need to find her essay."

"Sam burned the hard copies, but there should still be a file on her computer."

"Then let's find it," I stated.

Kylan followed me out of my dorm and across the quad. It was early morning and no one was around. The storm clouds from last night seemed darker now and churned overhead. Thunder rumbled in the distance.

"How are we getting into her room?" Kylan asked. "We don't have a key, and it'll be warded from uninvited visitors."

"I'm taking Wards 101, and we learned last week that when a person dies, the ward defaults to the family members. The ward will let me through, as long as I can get past the lock."

Kylan held the door open for me as we stepped inside the building. "How exactly are you going to do that?"

I approached Luna's room. "The way Emerson taught me. Keep watch."

I knelt in front of the door and pulled two bobby pins from my hair. I never condoned Emerson's special interests, but I'd listened when he talked about lock picking, because I wanted him to know I cared. I never thought I'd be the one breaking and entering.

I wiggled the bobby pins the way Emerson taught me, until the lock slid open. Kylan and I ducked into the room before we could be spotted. I ignored the way my body shuddered at the memories of last night, pushing past it to search for Luna's laptop. I hurried over to the desk in the corner, where her printer was. All I found were stacks of blank printer paper and a few sheets of photo paper.

Kylan searched the bedroom, but he found nothing. "The police must've taken her laptop as evidence."

I slumped to my knees in front of Luna's altar. "Sam and Luna were working on that essay together, which means it's tied to the case. The police are never going to release it to the public."

Kylan knelt beside me. "Maybe we don't need Luna's essay to learn what happened to Emerson. If she could uncover clues on her own, then so can we."

I frowned. "You heard Sam. The spell they did on his bones could only be done on Halloween. We'd have to wait another year to replicate Luna's research, and that's *if* the spell worked again. Who's to say it won't lose potency the longer his bones have to decay? I just know we don't have the full story, and it's not fair to Luna or Emerson."

I picked up one of the amethyst crystals I'd used in my séance the day before. Amethyst was used to enhance intuition and create a deeper connection to spirit. I hated that it hadn't worked, because if Luna were *here*, she could provide answers. If I could say goodbye, maybe this wouldn't hurt so bad.

Sadly, I opened the small drawer in her altar to put the crystals away. I stopped in my tracks.

Inside the drawer sat a tattered piece of paper that looked like Luna had ripped it from one of the old spellbooks in the library. Luna would *never* defile a piece of history, so this was strange. On the top of the page in Luna's handwriting read the word, *Murder Weapon*. My fingers quivered as I pulled the page from the drawer and began reading.

One flaming candle lit
Two drops of blood given
Speak these words on Samhain
"Where is the secret hidden?"

"Halloween's roots go all the way back to the Celtic festival of Samhain," I remarked. "This is another spell that can only be performed on Halloween."

"Is it the one she used on Emerson's bones?"

I shook my head. "This is different from what Sam described. It's a tracking spell. But this is old magic. The coven hasn't resorted to blood magic in over a century. Look what she wrote here."

Kylan took the page. "*Murder weapon*? Luna really believed Emerson was murdered."

"The question is… did she figure it out?" I looked back into the drawer, only to notice something I hadn't seen the first time. I reached inside to pull out an ancient brass skeleton key. I could feel the magic pulsing through it.

Kylan tilted his head curiously. "That looks like something from the Records Hall."

"I think it *is*. I learned about these keys in Wards 101.

They're ancient spells magically enchanted to break wards. They're really hard to make. The coven only has a few of them."

"Then what's Luna doing with one of them?"

"She's interning at the Records Hall. She must've taken it."

Kylan reached for the key to inspect it. "So… Luna was tracking down a murder weapon, and to get to it she had to get past a ward?"

Luna wasn't the kind of person to break the rules. It was odd she'd have either of these items in her possession. Which meant she was close to solving the case. I knew it.

I stood on shaky knees and took a step back. The instant my foot landed, color flashed across my vision. It happened so quickly I couldn't quite make sense of what I'd seen. All I caught was a chestnut brown and thought it might be a tree.

"What is it?" Kylan must've noticed my shocked expression.

"I'm getting something." I glanced down to see that I was standing right where Luna's body had fallen last night. I quickly jumped several feet away.

Kylan glanced between me and the empty space between us. His features fell when he realized why I'd jumped. "This is where you found her?"

I nodded solemnly. To come back here at all was difficult, but to stand exactly where she fell… it seemed like a betrayal, like I might somehow defile the last moments of her life by stomping out her memory.

Kylan placed a gentle hand on my shoulder. "If it's too much, you don't have to do this."

I stared down at the spot where she died. The police had collected all their evidence, so there wasn't a chalk outline like in the movies. But it seemed like there should be, because that's how it *felt*.

I stood inches away from where she died, but it seemed that standing *right there* triggered my visions. As long as I didn't touch that spot, I wouldn't have to witness her death again.

But if I didn't take this step, I may never uncover the truths that Luna had died for. She'd worked so hard to figure out what really happened to Emerson, and if I walked away now, then her death would be reduced to merely a jealous rage, and her commitment to uncovering the truth would be forgotten.

There were other psychics in the coven, but none as connected to this case as I was. If I was receiving a vision, then there was a spirit trying to send me a message—a message meant only for me. All I had to do was trust that it would lead me in the right direction.

"I want to do this," I told Kylan.

I took a step forward, plunging myself head-first into what I feared may be a life-altering vision. Chestnut brown filled my senses, along with the slight scent of something burning. The sensations were gone as quickly as they came.

Kylan waited patiently, but he didn't prod.

I knelt down and splayed my hand over the floor. "I need to get closer to her."

I didn't know where the thought came from, but it felt true. Slowly, I lowered myself to the ground. I trembled from head to toe, as if simply existing in this space might subject me to the same curse that killed Luna. I lay back in the same position I'd found her in last night.

Then something changed. I felt a calmness wash over me, like lying here only brought me closer to her life, rather than her death.

An image flashed across my mind again, only this time I caught sight of an intricate swirling pattern. "I'm getting something. Kylan, grab the photo paper from Luna's desk."

Kylan rushed across the room. "What are you going to do?"

"Thoughtography," I told him. "I can't get a clear enough picture in my mind. I have to imprint the vision onto photo paper."

Kylan slipped the paper under my hand, and I pressed my palm down as the vision flitted through my mind again. Magic swelled up from my toes and out my arms, the warmth of it settling into the paper.

Kylan gasped. My eyes shot open, and I sat upright. As I lifted the paper, my stomach sank. The image depicted a door with a starry swirl pattern carved into it… the exact door we'd seen last night at the Woodfield residence.

I swallowed hard. "Luna tracked something down to Sam's house? I don't understand how that could be related to Emerson's death."

"Sam could've been hiding evidence from her," Kylan theorized.

"That tracks," I agreed. "If he had something that could

crack the case, they'd finish their essay and wouldn't need to work together anymore. Sam was obsessed with her, so he wanted to keep her around as long as possible. Hiding evidence meant she'd have to keep investigating with him."

Kylan's brows shot up. "If she found out he was hiding the murder weapon, she wouldn't trust him anymore. She'd be afraid of him. I'd have wanted to be removed from the assignment, too. That must've been what freaked her out last night."

I stood and straightened my spine. "We have to go back, Kylan. We need to find out what Sam was hiding."

"We should go to the police," he argued.

I shook my head. "I don't trust the sheriff. If we go to him, we risk him covering up evidence for his kid. You heard him last night—he's going to try to get Sam out of this. For all we know, Sam's already told his dad what he's hiding. We have to do this before the evidence goes missing. Luna and Emerson are gone, so we have to finish this for them."

Kylan nodded in agreement. "Let's give our friends the closure they deserve."

CHAPTER 11

We took Kylan's car to Proctor Drive. It didn't look like anyone was home, so we rounded the side of the house to the back again. It'd started raining, and the thick raindrops helped conceal us as we snuck through the neighborhood.

I felt a magical barrier press against us when we reached the backyard. It was like a bubble, keeping us from getting any closer.

"There's a ward that wasn't here last night," Kylan remarked.

"Good thing we have this." I pulled the skeleton key I'd brought along from my pocket. I pointed it toward the magic, and the bubble seemed to pop instantly. We raced toward the back door, but found it locked.

"Stand back!" Kylan lifted his wand. We had to get that evidence before anyone returned home, which meant we couldn't waste time trying to get in unnoticed.

A powerful spell shot out the end of his wand, shattering the door to pieces. Glass rained across the kitchen floor, but we paid it no mind as we rushed inside. Rainwater soaked our clothes and pooled at our feet. Outside, thunder rocked the skies.

I ran to the door with the stars on it and twisted the handle. Behind it, we found a dark, descending staircase. The stairs creaked under our weight as we entered the basement into the center of a large room. I came to an abrupt halt when we reached the bottom of the stairs.

Before us stood a fully-stocked alchemy lab with a long table stretching across one wall, complete with cauldrons and potion vials in all different sizes. Hundreds of bottles lined various shelves. The contents of each vial shared the same color—a dark, maroon liquid reminiscent of red wine.

The wind knocked out of me. "This is the potion Emerson stole from the police officer, which he drank the night of the Enchanted Ball. The officer that stopped him that night must've been the sheriff!"

Kylan began recording the evidence on his phone. "This is the murder weapon Luna tracked down. This potion killed him. Why would someone need to brew this much poison?"

I approached a spell book that lay open beside the largest cauldron. At the top of the page read the words, *Power Enhancement*. "It's not poison," I realized. "It's a potion that boosts your magic. The sheriff must be using this to make himself stronger, but Emerson was still young when he died. A surge of magic would've overloaded his system. Emerson died of the Deluge, caused by this potion, and then fell from the balcony once his life had already ended."

I read over the ingredients and shuddered when I saw that it required the bones of an earth-bound ghost.

Kylan peered over my shoulder. "This is forbidden magic. Defiling someone's bones before they've moved on could trap their spirit here. It's sick."

Thunder cracked overhead, and the pouring rain grew louder.

"Why would Sam investigate this if his father was involved?" I wondered.

"Unless Sam didn't know until they got deeper into the project," Kylan pointed out. "If anyone found out the sheriff was brewing this potion, he'd be in prison for life. That must be why Sam hid the evidence."

"And why Luna asked to be taken off the project," I remarked. "She wasn't just scared of Sam. She was afraid to go to the police, because she discovered the sheriff caused Emerson's death. Sam didn't destroy the essay copies because they reminded him of Luna. He destroyed them to erase the evidence of his father's involvement."

"We have to talk to Professor Wilde," Kylan insisted. "We can't trust the police, but she'll know what to do. We have what we need. Let's go."

We whirled toward the exit, but my heart stalled when we found a tall, shadowed figure standing there. The storm outside was so loud we hadn't heard the stairs creak.

Sheriff Woodfield aimed his wand at us. "You won't be going anywhere."

Kylan and I flicked our wands at the same time, but the sheriff had already blasted a spell in our direction. A flash of magic slammed into Kylan's chest, and he flew off his feet. His body slammed into a shelf so hard that his skull cracked the shelf in half. Kylan slumped to the ground, and potion vials shattered all around him. The potion leaked across the floor, mixing with the thickness of Kylan's blood pooling from a wound on his head. He didn't move.

"NO!" I wailed, the heartbreaking cry echoing through the room.

Tears sprang to my eyes, and I staggered back to catch myself against the tabletop. When Kylan suggested we investigate Luna's death, I'd had a moment where I pictured him dead. At the time, I thought it'd only been my imagination. Now, I feared it was a premonition.

One I couldn't undo.

I didn't have a chance to process it before the sheriff aimed his wand at me. Instinct kicked in, and I ducked his incoming spell. It slammed against the wall, shattering bottles behind me. My head spun as I sought an exit in a desperate attempt to survive. All I could do was lunge beneath the stairs for cover.

"Oh, no you don't, you little bitch," he sneered.

The sheriff reached out, but I slipped back before he could grab me. I frantically blasted a spell in his direction. It didn't do any damage, but it knocked his wand out of his hand and bought me the second I needed. I kicked over several storage boxes as I bolted from beneath the staircase on the other side, then sprinted up the stairs.

His hand clamped around my ankle, and I tripped, clipping my chin against the stairs. My wand clattered down the stairs and onto the basement floor far below me. Heart pounding in absolute terror, I flipped over to find the sheriff's fuming gaze glaring up at me from beside the staircase. I didn't stop to think. I slammed my free foot against his face as hard as I could.

Bone crunched, and he cursed. I slipped from his grasp and scampered upstairs, running faster than I ever had before. I raced for the glass door Kylan and I had come through, but all the broken glass was gone. The door appeared as if it'd never been shattered in the first place. It seemed the sheriff had used some repairing spell to fix it. I yanked on the door handle, but the door wouldn't budge, even when I disengaged the lock.

My whole body rocked in fright. I whirled around for another exit, only to find the sheriff stumbling out of the basement to block my path. Blood dripped from his broken nose, but he was frightening as hell when he pulled himself to his full height. He was much taller than me, with wide shoulders and big muscles.

I shrank back, until my shoulders pressed into the cool glass behind me. Outside, the storm raged and the wind howled. The rain was so thick now that I couldn't see the neighbor's houses. Even if I screamed, I wouldn't be heard. I was just a first-year student, up against one of the most powerful and corrupt warlocks in the coven. I didn't stand a chance.

The sheriff waved his hand, summoning a long, thick rope from somewhere in the house. It flew down the hall and wrapped around me at his command. It happened so fast that I barely knew what was happening.

The rope curled around my arms like serpents striking for a kill. At the same time, the rope wove around the rungs of a kitchen chair, then yanked me into the seat. The cord slithered around me, until my arms and legs were secured tightly to the chair. I struggled against their hold, but they tightened like a noose. I'd never seen magic like this, as if the rope had a mind of its own.

Tears streaked my cheeks, and my voice trembled. "What is this?"

He gave a dark smirk. "Just a little spell I came up with —a rope soaked in a potion so potent it responds to the will of the most powerful spellcaster around."

I choked back my sobs, because now I was just *pissed*. "I saw your potion in the basement. Your power is a lie."

"It's not a lie if I've created the potion on my own. I'm gifted in alchemy, and I found a way to make more power out of it."

"At the expense of others' souls!" I snarled. "Bone magic is forbidden."

Sheriff Woodfield ignored the accusation and crossed the kitchen to the stove. "This magic was necessary. How do you think I became sheriff? Not by my average alchemy magic, that's for sure. I needed something more to show people how great I am."

He turned on the burner, then pulled a cauldron from the cupboard and placed it there. "It's a shame you didn't listen to me and leave your cousin's investigation to the professionals, Miss Graves. Fitting, your name is, because a grave is exactly where I plan to send you."

"You'll be caught," I spat. "Emerson and Luna are already dead. Add Kylan and me to the death toll, and they'll catch both you and your son!"

The sheriff gave a wicked laugh. "Who exactly is going to catch me? I've altered two investigations now. I can do it again—as many times as it takes to keep the secret of my power from getting out."

"Altered the investigations?" I repeated, then I realized what he meant. "The spell you did to reveal Luna's cause of death… that was all a lie? Luna never cast the curse."

He reached into the cupboard to pull down ingredients, then started tossing them into his cauldron. "Of course it was fabricated, same as when I cast the spell on your Hawthorne friend."

I thought he'd shown me how Luna died out of sympathy, but he did it deliberately to keep me from causing any trouble.

"With the magical boost from my potion, I'm strong enough to manipulate the spell to show people what I *want* them to see," he said.

"You were at the Enchanted Ball the night Emerson died. I remember you. You made everyone believe he jumped, just so no one would investigate the potion he'd drunk and find out you were a fraud! Too much magic can kill a person. How come the potion hasn't killed you yet?"

"It takes time to build a tolerance to the extra magic,

time your stupid little friend didn't have. I've been brewing this potion for years."

"So you killed Emerson, then let your son handle Luna?" I accused.

He stirred his potion on the stove. "I didn't kill your friend Emerson. I only covered up the cause of death. No one was supposed to find out I faked it, and they wouldn't have if that little bitch didn't come snooping."

"So, you're just fine with your son being a murderer?"

The sheriff whirled around. "Sam didn't kill Luna. *I* did. Sam knew nothing until you mentioned how *that boy* stole a potion from an officer, then told him about the hockey mask."

I recalled the hockey gear on the table last night. I figured it must've been Sam's, but now I realized it was the sheriff's. He'd been the masked man Kylan had witnessed leaving Luna's dorm.

The sheriff knelt in front of me, speaking in a mocking tone. "Sam told me all about that meeting you had in the Torture Chamber. He put two and two together, then came home to destroy the essay that would incriminate me. But when you caught him in the act, he thought he was saving me by confessing."

"Your son must really love you," I sneered. "I can't imagine why he'd stand up for someone so heartless."

Sheriff Woodfield stood, then scoffed. "Sam's pathetic. I always taught him to be the strongest one in the room, but making up that story about being in love with that girl and confessing was the weakest thing he could do. He claimed everyone called him the creepy guy anyway, so he might as well lean into it to save his poor old dad. Stupid kid. He should've killed you both."

"But Luna was here with Sam last night," I said, thinking of the tracking spell she'd used to find what killed Emerson.

"Luna came on her own while Sam was at Haunted Halls. Somehow, she broke my wards to trespass into my house."

That must've been how Kylan and I got inside so easily last night. The wards had already fallen, and the sheriff hadn't reinforced them until this morning.

Everything we assumed about Sam was wrong. He wasn't in love with Luna, and he'd been nowhere near her after their spell in the cemetery. Everything I learned fell into place. Luna and Sam had gone to the cemetery for research, where they learned that Emerson had a potion in his system at the time of death. Afterward, Sam went to Haunted Halls while Luna must've snuck into the Records Hall to continue her research, but the tracking spell she found had to be completed on Halloween, so she couldn't wait. She continued her research alone.

Luna tracked the murder weapon down to Sheriff Woodfield's address, and brought the skeleton key along to break his wards. She messaged Professor Wilde just before she broke into the Woodfield house and found the evidence in the basement. When she realized the connection to the sheriff, she begged Professor Wilde to drop the essay. Going to the police would put her life in danger. She couldn't tell Professor Wilde what she found, either, as it would risk her life as well.

Luna hadn't been acting jumpy lately because she was scared of Sam. She was distracted by the case and focused on getting answers.

"I was alerted when the wards fell and tracked the intruder to her dorm, where I learned what she knew and killed her so she couldn't talk," the sheriff admitted.

"And you just left her there?" I spat.

"I intended for someone to find her and stage it as an accident. You were supposed to accept the story, but instead you went digging," he growled.

"You were the one who burned her essay, then you took her laptop as evidence, so you could destroy that copy, too! I handed my phone over to you—all those recordings, just so you could destroy that evidence. You didn't even bring Sam back to the station last night, did you?"

The sheriff tilted his head innocently. "Why would I? Sam did nothing wrong. I merely sent him out of town for a few days to give him a good alibi. Wouldn't want him around for what's to come. What I can't figure out is how *that bitch* got past my wards, or how you managed, for that matter."

I stilled. Something in my eyes must've given myself away, because the sheriff's gaze dropped to my pocket. He lunged for me, but the harder I tried to wriggle away, the tighter the rope squeezed me to the chair.

He ripped the skeleton key from my pocket and held it up. "So that's how you little shits got into my house!"

I realized something else then that should've raised red flags at the time, but I hadn't noticed. "You came home during the witching hour last night. You should've been out celebrating with the rest of the coven."

"I didn't have a chance to reinforce my wards before you and your boyfriend broke in, but my ward magic lingered just enough to alert me of intruders."

"How'd you manage to hide all this from other psychics in the coven?"

He shrugged nonchalantly. "The dead don't want to talk when they know what's at stake. I could still use their bones to brew my potion, and no one wants to be stuck here forever with unfinished business."

"So you're a grave robber, too? Or do you kill *all* your victims?"

"I told you I didn't kill the Hawthorne kid," he snapped. "Your cousin had to go so no one would find out about my potion, and you'll be lying in a grave beside hers. Who else did you tell about all this!?"

"They'll find you! Four deaths is going to raise red flags."

"I can spin it however I want. *The poor young girl who lost her friends goes for a drive, and in the midst of her grief loses control and runs off the road, killing both herself and the passenger.*"

I scoffed. "They'll never buy that lame excuse. You got away with covering up Emerson's death because everyone wants to believe the depressed kid would rather die than turn his life around, but not every sad person wants to kill themselves."

He turned his back on me to stir his potion again. "That kid didn't have a future."

"He had a bright future, so bright it would outshine anything you've ever done! He was smart and funny, and he would've made a great enchanter one day, but you and your illegal potion took that from him. You might've had everyone convinced then, but they won't believe you now!"

The sheriff dipped a ladle into his potion. "I'm the sheriff. They'll believe whatever I tell them."

He approached me, the potion bubbling in his hand.

I squirmed in my seat. "What is that!?"

"Oh, just a little spell to compel you to do as I say. You'll get in the car you drove here in, and you'll run it off the road, whether you want to or not."

I turned my head away from him. "Why not just compel me to forget?"

The sheriff grabbed my hair, yanking my head back painfully. "That'd make this a lot easier, wouldn't it? The mind is a tricky thing, Miss Graves. Magic can manipulate your behaviors short-term, but something as long-lasting as memory can't be tampered with."

"This potion can't be legal!"

He threw his head back in laughter. "You act like I give a shit about the law. As sheriff, I'm above it. Now *drink*."

I clamped my mouth shut tightly, but he squeezed my jaw so hard I thought the bone might snap. My jaw hinged open against my will, and he shoved the potion inside, sloshing hot liquid over my cheeks and down my front. I wasn't sure what it tasted like, because the potion was so hot that it burned my tongue, instantly forming blisters.

Magic swelled upward, filling my body with a potent energy. It wasn't from the potion. His attack lit a fire within me, and somehow I just *knew* what I had to do. The following second flashed through my mind before it happened, and I saw myself falling. I couldn't say it made any sense, but I didn't question it. Instead of swallowing, I spat the boiling potion back in his face. He reeled back as the hot liquid burned his eyes.

"Bitch!" he screamed.

With his eyes clamped shut from the pain, he blindly lunged for me. I threw my shoulders to the side, gaining enough momentum to knock the chair over. A loud *snap* filled the air. The impact was hard enough to splinter the wood, separating the back from the base. The sheriff tripped over the feet of the chair, hitting his head on the edge of the table.

The broken chair caused the rope to loosen enough that I wriggled free. I scrambled to my feet, silently praying that he'd stay down long enough for me to escape. I backpedaled toward the hall.

Then I noticed the rope wiggling in his direction. He jumped to his feet, but the rope was already curling around his leg, like vines growing around his body. He blinked the potion out of his eyes, then looked down at the rope that had turned on him.

"How…?" he started.

I didn't know how I did it, but it was as if the rope had answered my prayer. Then I recalled what he said about its magic. "You said the rope responds to the will of the most powerful spellcaster around. You think that potion in the basement makes you strong, but strength isn't about how much magic you have—it's how you use it. You brewed that potion because you never believed that your power was enough, and that's where we're different."

The rope curled around his arms, pinning them to his sides. He tried to reach out to cast a spell, but the rope yanked his hand back. It squeezed him so tight he could hardly get the words out. "You're just a… first year student… with some party tricks."

"I'm a psychic," I stated proudly. "I have access to knowledge you never will, and that's where you underestimated me. You thought you could bury your secrets, but you didn't account for *me* getting involved. You thought my intuition meant nothing, because you yourself don't know how to trust your own power. I trust myself, and I believe in my magic. Now, the whole coven will know the truth."

He struggled against his bindings. "You aren't stronger than me. I covered up Emerson Hawthorne's cause of death, and I killed Luna Graves. I'll do the same to you—"

The sheriff cut off abruptly as a spell spun across the room and slammed into the back of his head. His eyes rolled back into his skull, and he collapsed to the ground, unconscious. I stared down at his body in shock.

Slowly, I lifted my gaze to see Kylan bracing himself against the basement door, his wand still raised and pointed right where Sheriff Woodfield had been standing. Blood matted in his hair, and the deep red of the power enhancing potion stained his clothes. His features were starkly pale, but he was *alive*. I rushed across the room and caught him just before he collapsed. I lowered him to the ground as he slumped against me.

"Kylan, we have to move," I urged. "The sheriff could wake any second."

"I already… called the police," he rasped. "They're on their way."

The last of the rumbling thunder faded, replaced by something I never thought would bring me hope. What once signaled death now filled me with a sense of relief.

In the distance came the sound of blaring sirens.

I helped Kylan to his feet and supported him as we stumbled out of the house. The storm had slowed to a drizzle, and I could see clearly down the street now as police cruisers and an ambulance sped up to the house. Emergency response crews swarmed us and helped Kylan into a stretcher.

A man with a mustache approached Kylan, while several other officers ran into the house. I recognized the deputy from the crime scene last night, though that seemed so long ago now. "Are you the one who called?"

"Yes." Kylan pulled his phone from his pocket. "I've got proof of everything I told the dispatcher. The sheriff confessed to murder. I got it on video."

The deputy appeared wholly shocked, but there was something else there, a crack in his faith that I witnessed crumble all at once when Kylan replayed the end of the video.

The sheriff's voice rang out through the speaker. "*I*

covered up Emerson Hawthorne's cause of death, and I killed Luna Graves."

The deputy looked horrified, but quickly pulled himself together. "You're both safe now. The sheriff is not above the law, and he will face trial. With a confession like that, we're looking at a lifetime sentence."

The EMTs looked Kylan over while the deputy asked me a few questions. I answered the best I could, but it was obvious I was really shaken up. He was kind and didn't press too hard, but I was prepared to tell them everything if it meant locking Sheriff Woodfield away for good.

The deputy dismissed me, but as soon as I saw them dragging the sheriff out of the house with his hands magically secured behind him, I ran across the lawn toward him.

"You all work for *me*," the sheriff spat. "I demand you let me go."

"I'm afraid the judge would disagree," an officer replied. "You have a lot of explaining to do regarding the potion in your basement."

The officers opened the back of a police cruiser, but the sheriff caught sight of me as I approached. "It was her!" he cried. "She planted the evidence to frame me!"

I crossed my arms. I wanted to see the look in his eyes when he realized he couldn't hurt anyone else ever again. "It's over, Sheriff Woodfield. There's no more denying what really happened. It's as you once told me: *The evidence will reveal the truth.* And you can't bury that truth any longer."

The sheriff's face fell, but he didn't get a chance to

respond before the officers shoved him into the vehicle and slammed the door behind him. The siren blared as they drove him away.

I approached Kylan in the back of the ambulance once the cruiser had disappeared down the street. They must've decided he didn't need the stretcher, because he sat in the back with his feet dangling above the pavement. A blanket draped his shoulders. EMTs worked on cleaning up the wound on his head, but the officers ignored us as they dragged piles of evidence out of the house. Kylan held a large potion vial and sipped it slowly. It shimmered and glowed white, like the healing potion he'd brewed me last night.

"How are you doing?" I asked him.

He lifted the potion bottle. "A lot better, thanks to this."

He offered me a drink, and the burns in my mouth melted away.

I reached up to brush his hair from his eyes. Staring into those icy blue irises seemed like a miracle. I couldn't look away. "You hit your head really hard. I thought you were dead."

"I thought so, too," he admitted. "The EMTs said it's not too bad, that even the smallest head wounds bleed profusely."

"Kylan, you were *knocked out*. You could have a concussion."

"I'm *fine*," he insisted.

The EMT behind him cut in. "We'll see what the doctor says once we get you to the hospital. You have three minutes." She left the ambulance to give us a moment of privacy.

Kylan noticed me shivering and wrapped his arm around me, dragging me close beneath the blanket. The weight of everything that happened seemed to melt away, and I found myself instinctually resting my head against his shoulder. There were no anxious butterflies dancing in my stomach or heat rising to my cheeks—only a sense of absolute peace, like this was exactly where I was meant to be. It felt so strange in the wake of all this.

Kylan sighed, like he too found relief in our proximity. "I was thinking after the hospital, we could go to the river to throw some petals in and say goodbye to Luna the way we said goodbye to Emerson. If it's not too much."

"It'll be perfect," I told him. "I always thought it wasn't enough that Emerson didn't come back to say goodbye to us, but I never really understood that maybe he *couldn't*. We work so closely with spirits, but there's still so much about life after death that we don't understand. Luna couldn't speak to me directly, but through my visions she gave me everything she could. In a way, even though she couldn't cross realms, I think that was her way of saying goodbye."

Kylan chuckled lightly. "What a way to say goodbye."

"It was right for me, though. It's going to be hard to move on, but it would've been impossible if Emerson's and Luna's stories were left untold. This was all really scary, and I didn't want to follow my intuition, but in the end it was worth it because we uncovered the truth, and that's what my clairvoyance is all about, isn't it? Now Emerson and Luna get to rest in peace."

Kylan squeezed my hand. "We'll say goodbye whenever you're ready."

"We can go this afternoon. I have to visit my family first. I'm sure they've been trying to contact me all morning, but the sheriff took my phone. I need to let them know I'm okay."

Kylan pressed his lips to the top of my head—out of habit, I think. "Take all the time you need. I'll be here waiting… if you want me to."

I drew away to look him in the eyes, those eyes that felt so much like home. This time, I allowed myself to fall into them completely. "You don't have to keep waiting for me, Kylan. I'm right here. You were right, and I pushed you away because I was scared of losing you. But the truth is, my intuition tells me we belong together, and I'm not going against my intuition again."

His eyes lit up. "So, you want to try again?"

I lifted my hand to the side of his face, caressing his warm skin. "I want to do it right this time. I can't abandon myself when things get hard, and I won't abandon us, either. You were right, and I'm not the kind of girl to play small. I need to pursue psychic studies to become an Intuit, like I always talked about. And when it comes to us? I'll put in whatever effort it takes to make this work. I don't know where our paths are going, but I know wherever they lead, I'm meant to take this journey with you."

Kylan leaned toward me, and I closed the distance between us. Our lips connected, and passion unlike any I'd felt before surged between us. I could feel my magic coiling around me, swirling up from the ground and circling

Kylan in a sweet embrace. His magic did the same to me, and I felt the sincerity of his affection drawing me in.

My lips parted, and Kylan's hand settled on the back of my neck as our desire for one another swelled. I could've sworn the ground fell from beneath us, and we were either falling or floating—though I wasn't sure of which one. It was wholly terrifying and exhilarating at the same time. I wasn't sure how it could be both, but whichever it was, I knew that as long as Kylan was at my side, I wanted to be a part of it.

The kiss ended far too soon, and our breaths became shallow as we pressed our foreheads against one another.

"I won't question myself again," I promised breathlessly.

"You're allowed to question yourself," Kylan replied. "Just make sure the answer you settle on is the one truest to you."

I had lost two people I loved dearly, and the separation would forever haunt me. But it didn't define the whole of me. I'd used my magic to uncover the most sinister truths in the coven. With this power, I had a lifetime of truths to discover. But in that moment, there was one that rang true above all others.

My inner power was to be trusted.

And that was a truth no one could ever deny me.

THE END

Read another fantasy novella by Megan Linski and Alicia Rades in *The Lost Sphinx*. Continue on to read the first chapter!

THE LOST SPHINX
CHAPTER ONE

Gianna

I could hear it rattling in my ears, inescapable, unavoidable, harboring the call of death. *Thump. Thump. Thump.* I was certain it was the pounding of my own heart pummeling against my ribs for all to hear, betraying my concealment in the darkness as the royal guards pursued me. But as I peered down the village streets, terror tightened in my veins as I saw what those treacherous guards were really doing.

The gallows. The guards were constructing them in the town square, getting them ready for some poor soul to swing at the end of the noose come daybreak.

If I had anything to say about it, there would be no one for them to hang.

I snuck from one alleyway to another beneath the cover of night, knowing that if I were caught anywhere near the jail where they were holding my friend, I too would meet a dark fate at sunrise. I prayed to the gods for a vision to help me sneak past the guards, but no insight came. I had to work carefully, or Deryn and I would both perish before the kingdom itself collapsed.

The streets were normally empty at this time of night, but peasants traded whispers through doorways and armored guards hunted for any signs of traitors. Hoofbeats clomped against the cobblestone. I sank deeper into the shadows, pressing my back to the cool stone of a nearby building.

"This way!" a man shouted. A dozen guards galloped by without a glance toward the alleyway, riding black horses that rolled their heads, exposing the whites in their eyes.

I clutched the sword in my hand tighter as I peered onto the street. The guards were past me now, but I'd have to sneak into the town square where more were gathered in order to reach Deryn's holding cell.

I'd never had to use a sword before, as my position in the temple under the Oracle required knowledge rather than physical strength. But I'd been training with Deryn since we were children. I often won our sparring sessions, despite the fact that he had formal practice from the most decorated knights at the palace, and I merely had his guidance to go by.

It wasn't *proper* for a psychic sorceress to wield a sword, but Deryn had insisted that it wasn't right for a young woman like me to grow up unable to defend herself. If only the townsfolk knew that Gianna Fairbriar was getting swordplay lessons in secret from Prince Deryn himself. What a scandal that would be. My light footing made it easy to sneak up unnoticed, and my agile movements gave me an advantage over their strength. I couldn't hesitate to kill my opponent, and I wouldn't— not when Deryn's life was on the line.

I pulled the hood of my cloak over my red hair, then crossed the road silently. Purple and gold banners swayed in the wind overhead. They'd been hung to celebrate the coronation that was supposed to happen today— a coronation that had been delayed by an assassination attempt.

Five days ago, King Severin passed away. As was customary, a funeral was held at the temple, and subjects from all over the kingdom came to pay their respects. The monarchy moved quickly to crown Prince Alion, the eldest of the three princes, as to not leave a gap in leadership.

Then this morning the second eldest brother, Prince Helis, had stabbed Prince Alion with a dagger in his dressing chambers before the ceremony could begin. Word had traveled quickly through the streets of Mystic Peak. No one could believe what Helis had done. Alion and Helis were twin brothers, but Alion was three minutes older, which made him first in line for the throne. In a jealous rage, Helis had tried to kill his brother to gain the crown. When the guards caught him in the act, Helis fled.

I could hardly believe it myself. I liked Helis growing up, though I hadn't spent as much time with him as I had Deryn. I was the same age as Deryn, who was the youngest prince at just twenty-one years old. After the king's death, something dark awoke within Helis that I prayed I'd never have to witness again, and Deryn was in danger because of it.

I shot a glance over my shoulder. The peaks of the temple's spires towered high above the other buildings. I shuddered to think of what I'd watched happen there earlier tonight.

Rana— the great sphinx and Oracle of the realm, and my mentor— was taken from the temple by none other than Prince Helis. I tried to stop it, but Helis and his supporters had taken her before I could do anything.

Rana was a powerful being. With the body of a lion, the head of a woman, and mighty feathered wings, she had far greater strength than any human. She was the most powerful psychic in the realm, and her visions held great power. But a single sphinx was no match against twenty strong guards and their unbreakable iron chains.

Rana was a gifted prophet, and though I trusted her visions with my life, such power could not be summoned by will. I knew Helis had captured Rana to try and force her to foresee the future, so he could use her to defeat Alion and rule over all. I feared the Oracle's gift wouldn't be enough to save her from the vengeful prince and his guards.

I'd run from the temple immediately to alert the monarchy and seek aid. On my way to the palace, I heard the whispers. Prince Deryn had been arrested by Alion's men for allegedly aiding in the assassination attempt and helping Helis escape.

I knew better, and I didn't need a vision to prove it. Deryn was my closest friend. He would never harm one of his brothers, let alone go along with kidnapping Rana, who meant so much to me. Deryn was innocent, and Prince

Alion was reacting irrationally because he was afraid that if one brother could try to kill him, there was nothing stopping the other from trying.

Prince Alion could use his fear for good to barricade the city and protect his people from Prince Helis' nefarious plans. Instead, he was allowing his guards to stomp through the street in the middle of the night while actively readying the gallows to take the life of his innocent younger brother.

I sympathized with Prince Alion, but he was going about this all wrong. Now that Rana was missing, his royal consultants would be further misguided.

I didn't need Prince Alion to stop this, though. Rana was the most valuable prophet in our nation. If I could find where Helis took her, I could free her, and her visions would calm this chaos before the kingdom shattered to pieces.

Rana wasn't strong enough to stop Helis' guards, which meant I needed a creature stronger to help me free her. *No one* was stronger than a dragon shifter. I had to rescue Deryn, not just because I cared for him deeply, but because the fate of the entire kingdom relied on it.

I crossed another street, creeping closer to the town square. Far past the square and up the mountain, a formidable castle stood overlooking the kingdom. I thought of all the times I'd been there, running through the corridors with Deryn or playing in the caves within the mountain. If we couldn't rescue Rana and prove Deryn's innocence, then I feared neither of us would ever return to the palace.

Deryn would find somewhere else to go, I was certain. He'd be devastated to lose his family, but perhaps he'd find a home among the dragon shifters. He was the only shifter in the city, and he'd once confessed to me his desire to leave royal life behind to find other dragon shifters like himself. It would be a long, arduous journey, as no one knew where to find the other dragon shifters— not even the Oracle.

Deryn wouldn't care what it took. He would leave the kingdom and travel across the realm if he had to. He just needed a starting point guiding him toward the dragons, and then he would be gone.

It ached my heart knowing that I couldn't convince him to stay. I always pictured a future with Deryn, and I couldn't imagine a life without him. It wasn't unusual for royals to marry spiritual leaders, and for a long time, I thought that's where we were headed. Then Deryn confessed to me his desire, but we never began a courtship. We couldn't, knowing it would never work between us. Deryn knew I couldn't leave Mystic Peak. I'd grown up in the temple, training with the Oracle. One day, I would become an Oracle myself. My entire life and my future were here, so I couldn't be a part of Deryn's journey, leaving the realm in search of the dragon shifters.

I wanted nothing but the best for him, so it didn't matter how I felt about him or what my intuition told me. It wouldn't work between us because he wished to leave Mystic Peak, and I had to stay.

I shook off any thoughts of a potential future with Deryn, because all that mattered right now was the task in front of me. If I didn't pull this off, there wouldn't *be* a future for either of us— together or apart.

The town's jail was situated two streets over from the square. This road was relatively void of guards, but every now and then a group of them would come hurtling through on horseback. From here, the sounds of the gallows being constructed and the shouts of men only grew louder. I could see through gaps between the buildings that the square was full of weapons, including crossbows, longbows, and sharp swords. They even had a catapult, as if to scare off anyone who might protest Deryn's execution. I knew one wrong move would do me in.

I crept around the building toward the only entrance. Two guards stood on either side of the front door. The jail was rather benign, with stone walls and the smallest of barred windows high above the guards' heads. It wasn't a large structure, as long-term criminals were kept in the dungeons at the palace where the monarchy could keep a close eye on them. These cells in town were specifically reserved for those criminals awaiting execution.

I crouched in the shadows to assess the guards for weak points. These guards wore armor from head to toe, with heavy metal helmets and strong breastplates. The only way to get past them was a sure aim of my sword between the joints where one piece of armor met another— and I had to do it before they got a swing in of their own, because I had no armor to protect myself. I thanked the stars there were only two of them, but I couldn't take them both on at once.

I listened for the sounds of incoming soldiers, but I heard none. Lifting a rock I found at my feet, I tossed it as far as I could near the next alleyway.

The guards heard the clatter, and their hands immediately went to the swords on their hips.

"What was that?" one of them demanded.

"Someone's lurking nearby." The second guard sounded certain. "I'll go check it out."

The second guard approached the abandoned alleyway I'd thrown the rock toward. That's when I sprang from the shadows, coming at the first guard from the side. He caught sight of me and lifted his sword, but I'd already anticipated his reaction, and I was faster than he was. The tip of my sword jabbed upward, straight into the narrow gap beneath his breastplate.

The man gave a pained grunt, and blood spurted from his abdomen and onto the street. I yanked my blade from his flesh before his knees hit the ground. His armor clanked against the cobblestone from behind me as I raced toward the second guard.

The guard had heard the commotion and came running back, but I was already swinging my sword when he sprinted out of the alleyway. My heavy weapon clanged against his helmet, sending it flying off his head. He swung at me, but I ducked out of the way and rolled across the ground. His sword connected with the street merely an inch from where I'd landed. Perhaps the stars had heard my prayers after all.

In one swift motion, I sprang back to my feet and used all my strength to swing my sword at the exposed skin on his neck. My blade cut through the delicate flesh there, and he gave a gurgle as he fell to the ground.

I didn't have time to feel remorse. I grabbed the keyring that hung off the guard's belt, then turned toward the jail and barged through the front doors.

In the cell at the end stood a lone figure, his hands wrapped around the bars and a startled look on his face. My heart swelled at the sight of Prince Deryn's hazel eyes and the familiar dark curls that fell across his face. His features softened when I yanked back my hood.

"Gianna." Deryn's voice sounded like a song. "What are you doing here? If you're caught, you'll be killed!"

I marched up to his cell, my sword still dripping with blood. "I know you're innocent, Deryn. I'm here to break you out."

Continue the story by reading The Lost Sphinx!

About the Author

Alicia Rades is a USA Today Bestselling Author of young adult and new adult paranormal novels. When she's not dreaming up magical stories, she's either binge-watching paranormal TV shows, meditating, or making crafts and cooking with her family. Her favorite tropes are small-town mysteries, witches, and magical academies set in the modern world. She has an unhealthy obsession with psychic characters and writes with a deck of tarot cards next to her computer.